PACK OF LIES

Book One of the Red Ridge Pack

by Sara Dailey and Staci Weber

www.BOROUGHSPUBLISHINGGROUP.com

PACK OF LIES
Copyright © Sara Dailey and Staci Weber 2014

ISBN: 978-1-941260-54-8

Digital edition by GoPublished
www.gopublished.com

To our friends and family; you know who you are.

You are my hunger
Bellowing from the deepest part of me
A forsaken howling, cracked and twisted
Wrapping me in rambling delight
To be without you, shall remove me completely
Laying me down in the shadow of yesterday's dusk
Blanketing this blooming instant, my craving locked in dusty arms
Leaving my vessel dripping in tears, my heart the faintest murmur
Wandering between exile and infinity, this professed crooked love

By Jordan Mantell

Table of Contents

PART I.
Allison's Story

Chapter 1

Chapter 2

Chapter 3

Chapter 4

Chapter 5

PART II
Allison, Kendall, and Cade

Chapter 6

Chapter 7

Chapter 8

Chapter 9

Chapter 10

Chapter 11

Chapter 12

Chapter 13

Chapter 14

Chapter 15

Chapter 16

Chapter 17

Chapter 18

Chapter 19

Chapter 20

Chapter 21

Chapter 22

Chapter 23

Chapter 24

Chapter 25

Chapter 26

Chapter 27

Chapter 28

Chapter 29

Chapter 30

Chapter 31

Chapter 32

Chapter 33

Chapter 34

Chapter 35

Chapter 36

Chapter 37

Chapter 38

Chapter 39

Chapter 40

Chapter 41

Chapter 42

Chapter 43

Chapter 44

Chapter 45

Chapter 46

Chapter 47

Chapter 48

Chapter 49

Chapter 50

Chapter 51

Chapter 52

Chapter 53

Chapter 54

Chapter 55

Chapter 56

Chapter 57
Chapter 58
Chapter 59
Chapter 60
Chapter 61
Chapter 62

PART I

Allison's Story

Chapter 1

ALLISON

"I said break it up, ladies!"

Principal Murphy's voice barely registered before someone grabbed me and pulled me away from the little bobble-head who was still swinging. With my vision still narrowed and my fists clenched, I tried to regain some sense of self-control as I shook off Coach Cole's grip on my arm. Coach gave me a sympathetic look and warned, "Not again, Alli! When are you going to learn?"

Glaring back and forth between us both, Principal Murphy ordered, "Miss Hades, my office, now! And Miss Wright… well, just go see the counselor again. I will get to you later."

I could still hear the principal griping at Tiffany as he led her toward the front office. This was not my fault this time. The wench had it coming.

I had barely taken a step inside the counselor's office before she laid into me. "Sit down, Miss Wright. Listen, I know you don't want to be here; no one wants to be here, but it's either me or Officer Daniels and trust me, you're better off talking to me," declared Mrs. Parker, the very young, very inexperienced guidance counselor at South Shore High School.

Definitely preferring to deal with this little pixy-stick rather than the school police officer—affectionately nicknamed Zero by the student body for his zero tolerance policy—I sat, but not because I was scared, only because I hoped she might go easy on me if I played nice. This wasn't my first visit.

As I watched Mrs. Parker open my file, adjust her reading glasses, and clear her throat; I found myself wondering when my file became so big that it needed to be held with both hands. I'm really not a bad kid.

Seriously. It was just that lately trouble seemed to be following me around.

Parker sat back in her chair and huffed as she heaved my file onto her desk. As my multitude of office referrals spread across the desk and onto the floor, she said, "Really Allison, three major fights this semester already? It's barely October. What on earth is going on with you?"

There it was. The million dollar question. I took a moment, just to make her think that I was thinking about *what on earth was going on with me*. I think it's safe to say that there was a lot going on with me, but surely she didn't think I was going to sit here and spill my guts to a guidance counselor, for Christ's sake. *How pathetic does she think I am?*

I counted slowly to ten in my head before I responded, "Nothing, I'm fine," and went back to picking at my nails. What exactly did she expect me to say? I could have said a hell of a lot. Like that every girl in this school suddenly seems to have a problem with me. That I can't go anywhere without them giving me dirty looks or making crude comments. And then there's my favorite. Apparently, I'm out to steal anyone's boyfriend that I come across, and therefore, I must be a slut.

What is with girls and the word "slut" anyway? Knowing I haven't had much experience with the opposite sex, I should just let it roll off my back, right? But slut is like the worst thing a girl can call another girl. And for some reason, the entire female body at South Shore High seems to be in agreement that I am, in fact, a complete and utter slut.

I wasn't going to tell Mrs. Parker what it had really been like for me for the past two months. She could just sit there, take her little notes, and pass my file on to the principal so that he could give me yet another consequence that I didn't deserve.

Parker looked at me over the top of her too-trendy reading glasses and admonished, "Look, Allison, you're going to have to do better than that. You are well on your way to the alternative high school, and the only reason you aren't there already is because you don't seem to be the instigator in all of this nonsense. But there has to be some reason why you were involved in three major fights, and who knows how many other minor altercations that weren't reported."

That did it. There was no way I was going to listen to her put this all on me. Yeah, I had planned to just sit there and listen to her "advice," but now she was acting like this was all my fault. So instead, like usual as of lately, I stood up, looked down on the pixy, and snapped, "Look, I don't know why, okay. I don't know why all of a sudden every girl in this school hates me. I don't know why guys that I have never even glanced at think that they can grab my ass in the hallway. I don't understand how people who I have been friends with for years don't want to talk to me or be seen with me in the cafeteria anymore. I have lost everyone, my best friend, my boyfriend, even the girls I have been friends with since elementary school. And I don't know why. Why don't you tell me? You tell me Mrs. Parker, you're the expert, right? Tell me why I don't have a single friend anymore except my brother."

I had no idea why or when it started, but tears were rolling down my face, and I was yelling at this poor lady who looked as shocked by my outburst as I was. So much for playing it cool. Now, I felt like I needed to apologize for putting that expression on her face. It's not really her fault that everything was so screwed up.

I took a deep breath, sat back down, and calmly said, "I'm sorry Mrs. Parker. That was out of line. I didn't mean to yell at you like that. It's just so frustrating. Everything is just kind of falling apart and I don't know what to do."

Mrs. Parker handed me a tissue and walked around her desk to sit in the seat next to me. She took off her glasses and said, "Honey… it's okay. And if you don't mind me being brutally honest, I *will* tell you why you have no friends, girlfriends at least."

Seriously? Wiping my mascara-smeared eyes, I nodded my head ready for her to enlighten me.

"Now, listen closely 'cause this is a life lesson," she said scooting a little closer to me.

"Are you listening?" She paused to make sure I was paying close attention. "Females can be catty, conniving, evil bitches. And for the most part, we don't like women who are better looking than we are," she admitted in hushed tones, as if someone nearby might hear.

I couldn't help but smile a little at Mrs. Parker, the sweet little guidance counselor saying "bitches."

"You may not have noticed or maybe you have, but you are certainly not the same young woman you were last year. You have changed, and even I have noticed the attention—good and bad—that you are getting because of it."

This lady can't be serious. "I'm sorry Mrs. Parker, but I don't buy it. My brother and I look just alike, and he has more friends than he can count. Nobody hates him, or spreads rumors about him, or starts fights with him. He's like Mr. Popularity around here."

"The rules are different for guys like your brother. Let me be honest with you," she said sitting back in her chair. "I promised myself I would never say this to a student, or my own children, for that matter. In fact, it's one of my pet peeves, but in your case I think it's actually true. They're jealous. All of them. Every girl and probably even a few teachers in this school. Jealously can do strange things to people."

I just stared at her like she had lost her mind, she continued, "Alli, you are taller, stronger, and more beautiful than any other girl in this school, and let's face it child, you have a killer body too. And to top it all off, you seem to be a genuinely nice person. Girls really hate people like you. You are their ultimate competition, and they know they don't stack up, so instead, they've evidently chosen to make your life miserable."

Wow, this woman was really nuts. How was I supposed to respond to that? *Yes, Mrs. Parker, I have noticed how hot I am and how great my tits and ass look lately. Jeez!* I always thought it would be great to be *that* girl, but for the record, it sucks.

"So what am I supposed to do about it?" I asked, hoping she just might have the answer I've been looking for.

"Well, there's not much you can do, dear. Hmmmm, let's see. Why don't we start with not hitting anybody?" she suggested with sarcasm oozing from her pores.

Yeah, now there's some advice I could use.

So I guess when some hussy is accusing me of trying to hit on her man, I'm just supposed to ignore it. Well, that was unlikely to happen any time soon.

Parker's you-know-I'm-right smirk was starting to piss me off. How could she think it would be that simple?

"But it's not my fault. They push me and push me until I can't take it. I seriously think they are trying to get me kicked out or something."

"Well, don't let them win. I know it sounds cliché Allison, but you need to be the bigger person and just walk away."

***

When I wandered out of Parker's office, the school secretary gave me an unsympathetic look as she informed me that my mom was here and had just gone in to see Principal Murphy. I could only imagine how that was going. I just hoped that I was still a student at South Shore come morning and not a new member of the Creek Alternative Education School.

Not wanting to sit in the office with the school secretary's opinionated glare, I politely requested that she let my mom know that I would be waiting in my car. The dismissal bell rang, and as I walked out to the parking lot, I carefully avoided all eye contact, trying to "be the bigger person" and all. With my eyes on the ground, I didn't see anyone coming until I ran right into the last person I wanted to see. I looked up startled, only to find, Julie, my ex-best friend. Her eyes shot up from her iPhone, and she said, "Oh… hey."

"Hey Julie. How ya been?" I asked, hoping she might stop to talk, but instead she just kept walking and finishing her text. I turned to watch her pass, feeling the familiar sting that still gets me even after all this time. How could she just forget how close we once were? It was by no means the first time I had tried to rekindle our friendship, and the outcome has always been the same.

I got in my car and turned the A/C on full blast. Leaning my head against the window, I closed my eyes and tried to focus on cooling down. It has been hotter than hell lately, everywhere I went, which is not entirely unusual in Texas, but it was weird. I didn't sweat. It was like I was hot on the inside. A fever maybe?

The more I thought about it, the more I was convinced that I was definitely coming down with something. It was not just being hot; my vision had been a little funny too. Not blurry or hazy or anything, just different. And on top of that, I kept getting these waves of nausea from all these funky smells in the air. I swear some people don't wear enough deodorant, and if I smell one more girl with vanilla body spray, I might just have to hurl.

Really… could life get any suckier? Not only was I a social pariah, but a sick one at that. There should be a rule or something that everything is not allowed to go wrong all at once. Right?

I was half-way to dreamland when my brother, Aiden, started pounding on the windshield.

"Yo, Balboa! I heard you kicked Tiffany Hades's ass. When are those dumb broads gonna learn not to mess with my little sis, huh?"

I opened the car door and got out, glad to see a friendly face, the only friendly face I knew lately.

"Tiffany is a dumb-ass, and she had it coming," I replied.

"Well, I can't exactly argue with that," he said as he threw his arm over my shoulder, leading me toward the gym.

"Come on, Al. Walk me to practice."

We walked in silence for a minute or so, and then with a heavy sigh, Aiden asked, "So, what are we gonna do about you? You can't keep beating up all the pretty girls. Who will I take to prom?"

"That's not funny, and it's not my fault. Her loser boyfriend grabbed my ass in the hall, and she just happened to be standing right there. Apparently, Tiffany saw that as my fault."

"Thomas? Thomas did what? What an asshat! He should know better than to mess with my little sis. I may just have to kill him now," Aiden said with a tough-guy smile.

I couldn't deny that Aiden had taken pretty good care of me since I went from something to nothing in no time flat. He was well aware that people talked mess about me constantly and have written me off the who's who list, but he didn't care what they thought. And he certainly didn't let anyone bad-mouth me when he was around.

Honestly, I didn't know what I would do without him. He was the closest friend that I have ever had, and currently my only friend, though that hadn't always been the case.

But as close as we are, Aiden and I are polar opposites. He's funny and outgoing, and of course, the most popular guy at every high school in the greater Houston area. There was even a rumor that he was nominated for homecoming king at our rival school, Bay Creek, which I had no doubt was true. He plays every sport, makes straight As, has more girls after him than he can handle, and is a good four inches taller than me, and I'm five foot ten. He has green eyes and dark brown hair instead of my hazel eyes and blonde hair, but we both have an olive complexion, yet somehow, I'm hated and he is adored.

Again, Aiden took a deep breath and said, "I don't know what to tell you, Al. Just don't let them get to you. Tiffany's an idiot, and everyone knows it."

"I know, but…"

"Just do me a favor? Don't get kicked out of school. Okay?"

He smiled at me, and took off into the locker room before I could tell him that it might be too late.

I turned around and headed back to my car, just in time to see one very angry mom heading straight toward me.

Chapter 2

ALLISON

Since arriving home, I had only one goal in mind—completely avoid my parents at all costs. Mom didn't say a word to me. Instead, she just stomped along with down-cast eyes until we arrived at my car, and then without a word, she stomped away toward her own. Not too sure what to think of that. She looked as though she had plenty to say, but for some unknown reason, evidently decided to hold off for a bit.

I, in turn, took it as an opportunity to race home before Mom could get there, and rush up to my room before I had to face her.

I had been shut in my safe-haven for over an hour without so much as a peep from anyone, which made me even more nervous. Mom rarely lets me do the whole leave-me-be-thing, and she was obviously upset after speaking to the principal. Maybe she was taking some time to cool off. Mom can be good at that sometimes.

Although, more often than not, when she's acting all patient she has an ulterior motive. Nine times out of ten, she'll leave me alone just long enough to make me think that maybe I got away with whatever it was that I royally screwed up, and then POW! She'll let me have it. I had no reason to believe that this time would be any different. Especially since this wasn't her first conversation with the administration about my behavior.

Trying to keep myself occupied, I grabbed the US Weekly from my nightstand and cranked up my iPod.

I had just taken my mind off of my impending doom when Aiden eased my door open and peeked inside. "Hey Al, just so you know I *was* knocking. Anyways, dinner is ready," he said, attempting to sound causal, as if I didn't realize I was about to have to face the wrath of mommy-dearest.

I looked up at him with a blank stare, even though I had clearly heard him, and put my iPod down.

When I didn't respond, he repeated, "I said dinner was ready."

"Great. I can't wait," I said sarcastically. "Did Mom say anything to you?"

He looked down at the floor without answering. What did that mean?

"Aiden! Did she say anything or not? You're freaking me out," I said as I slammed my magazine down on my bed.

"No, but I have a feeling that it's not going to be good. I mean this is your third fight. What do you think Mom and Dad are going to say? *Great job, Honey. Third time's a charm!*"

"Don't be a smart-ass, Ad," I said, and jabbed him in his ribs with my elbow on my way out the door. "Come on, let's get this over with."

***

I sat down at the dinner table with my eyes glued to the floor and waited for the fireworks to begin, but they didn't come. Instead, my dad acted like nothing happened. He even asked me nicely if I wouldn't mind helping him set the table, which, for some reason, made me feel even lousier about the trouble I had caused.

With the table set, there was nothing left to do but sit back down and endure whatever Mom had coming for me.

Is Principal Murphy going to kick me out of school?

What if my parents kick me out of the house?

What if they send me away to some school for screwed up teens, like the reform schools you see in movies?

I sat there, waiting, but no one said anything. We all ate dinner in what could only be described as a seriously uncomfortable silence. Five minutes, ten minutes, fifteen? No one spoke. Aiden hadn't even looked up from his plate. *What the hell?*

Dad had made steak, my favorite, and I couldn't even find it within myself to enjoy it. Maybe this was some new method of parenting Mom read about; make the kid feel so bad about herself that she never gets in any trouble at all.

Finally, the silence was broken.

"We are all going to have a talk after dinner, okay?" Mom said sounding a bit nervous.

Dad reached over to pat Mom's arm as if to comfort her, which made my stomach churn.

Shit! I am definitely going away. They are so kicking me out of school! I know it! Military school, here I come.

My mind reeled as I watched my parents talking with their eyes. I glanced back and forth between the two of them, and when I turned to Aiden to see how he was taking all of this weirdness, as usual, he seemed completely unfazed by any of it. I felt like shouting, "Hello? Earth to Aiden! Are you seeing this? Your sister is about to be booted out of school! Do you even care?"

I pushed the food around on my plate, no longer able to stomach it with the tension mounting in the air. The longer we sat at the table the more anxious I became. Finally, I couldn't take the suspense any longer and belted out, "Can we please just get this over with? I'm not really in the mood to puke up my steak and baked potato, and if someone doesn't tell me what is going on, it just might happen."

Mom and Dad froze and both suddenly looked as though they may puke as well. Their silence was all but killing me.

Aiden put down his fork and cleared his throat. "Ummm, should I leave? Do y'all want to talk to Al alone?" he asked.

Thanks a lot Ad. Way to be there for me, big bro.

Mom and Dad looked at each other once more. Then their eyes darted back and forth between Aiden and me before finally landing on the floor.

I stared at them both unable to believe that it had come to this. They couldn't even look at me.

"Just tell me!" I shouted. "You're sending me away, aren't you?" I asked, sure my number was up.

Finally, Mom opened her mouth to speak.

"No Alli, we are not sending you away. God, this is so hard. I'm not sure where to start," Mom mumbled under her breath.

Dad poured her another glass of wine and reassured her, "You can do this Lillian. They'll understand. They can handle it."

"Just say it, Mom. Whatever it is, I can take it," I said trying to sound convincing. Honestly, I wasn't ready for it. Whatever it was.

Mom scooted her chair out from under the table and turned toward Aiden and me, suddenly seeming a lot more confident. Taking a deep breath, she began, "Okay, several months ago, we started to notice that you were both changing. Physically. And obviously from what's been going on with Alli, emotionally too. God... I should have told you this a long time ago. Maybe you would have taken it better, especially you Al. I'm so sorry."

"What are you talking about Mom? You aren't making any sense."

"Just let her finish, Alli. This is important," Dad said.

Mom again looked back and forth between Aiden and me and finally admitted, "Okay, I'll just say it. I'm a werewolf and y'all will be too very soon. There, I said it. It's out."

Aiden and I looked at each other and busted out laughing. Had she lost her ever-loving mind?

"Hey Mom! Grrrrrrrr! Maybe you should lay off the wine before you sprout some back hair," Aiden somehow managed to say through his laughter.

I was doubled over, almost in tears, when Mom got up from the table and left the dining room without a word. Our laughter ceased when Dad threw his napkin on the table and stood up to surely chastise us, but his speech was cut short when an enormous, dark-brown wolf wandered into our dining room and bared its teeth at Aiden.

"Grrrrrrrrrrrrrr!" the wolf growled with fury.

Now it was Dad's turn to laugh as Aiden high-tailed it on top of the dining room table, screaming, "Holy shit! What the hell is that?"

Still smiling, Dad said, "That would be your mom, son, and no cussing at the dinner table."

I wasn't screaming or jumping on table tops. Instead, I was frozen in place, seemingly suspended in time. Dad was laughing, Aiden was shaking, and my mom...wolf...mom-wolf, whatever she was, was staring at us all with the same dark brown eyes she's always had. It was real. She was real. *Holy shit is right! My mom is a werewolf!*

Chapter 3

ALLISON

After the initial shock of Mom's little "announcement" settled in, my mom, no longer in her wolfie form, decided to tell us *the real* story of how Dad and her got together. The one that was supposedly going to explain all of this craziness and help us understand just how we ended up in this paranormal state of existence.

Mom took a moment to straighten her clothes before she began. "Well, you know the story of how your father and I met?" Mom asked.

Aiden and I nodded.

"It's all a lie. We didn't actually meet in church like we told you before. I'm sorry kids, but we couldn't exactly tell you the truth," she bluntly admitted.

"Holy shit, Mom. What else is a lie? Is he even our real father?" I asked without thinking first, which was probably not the best thing to do, but to be honest, I was completely appalled by the whole absurd situation.

"Your mouth, Alli. Jeez, we did not raise you to speak that way," my dad immediately scolded.

Tempted to get up from the table and storm away from this whole nightmare, I reminded myself to calm down and to breathe. I couldn't run from this. I needed to know what was in store for me now, now that I'm apparently not as human as I had previously thought.

After a few deep breaths, I said, "Okay, I'm sorry. I'm just a bit freaked out at the moment. Can you blame me?"

Mom patted me on the leg. "It's okay, honey. I know this is a bit hard to swallow."

"So what is the truth, Mom?" Aiden added sympathetically, playing the-good-son part.

"The truth? Oh God, where do I start?"

"How about the beginning, Mom," I suggested trying to keep the irritation out of my voice but failing miserably. I was riding a rollercoaster of emotions that I couldn't seem to get off of. I went from being a jerk to apologetic to a jerk again in no time flat, and I wasn't able to control it.

Mom gave me a snarky little smile before explaining, "When I was twenty-one, I went with some friends from my pack into town for a music festival."

"Wait, you had a pack, like a wolf pack? This is kinda cool, Mom," Aiden said.

"Shut up," Dad and I said in unison.

"Yes, I had a pack, but, if you don't mind, can I tell the story?" Mom paused for a moment to make sure we were listening. "So, we went to see this punk band that we had heard was pretty good."

"A punk band, Mom? Really?" I asked, surprised to hear that Mom would have actually liked that kind of thing, even that long ago.

"Hey, don't knock it. It beat the bluegrass bands that were there most nights. Anyway, there we were watching this really great band," Mom said as she winked at Dad, "when I saw your dad. He was the bass player. Our eyes met and… what can I say. It was love at first sight. I made my way up to the stage just as they finished their set to introduce myself, and, well, we ended up spending the entire night together after the show."

"Spent the night together, huh?" Aiden said before he smiled and winked at Dad.

Mom glared at him and said, "It wasn't like that, honey. It was the perfect night. We talked, and danced, and talked some more. After that night, I snuck off the estate whenever I could to see him because, you see, at the time, I was kind of engaged."

"What! Engaged? To whom?" I asked, astounded that my mom was engaged to someone else, someone I had never heard of, and that she was cheating on him with my father.

"Yes, sort of. Promised, really, to my pack's soon-to-be alpha. We dated for a long time, but see, we were friends and while I did care for him, I didn't love him, not like that anyway. The truth is that if we were to have gotten married, it would have been to strengthen the pack, not because we truly wanted to be husband and wife."

Dad reached out and grabbed Mom's hand, a sweet gesture that I'm sure Mom appreciated. Watching Dad be all husband-like, I couldn't decide which was harder to believe, that my mom was a werewolf, or that my dad was in a punk band. I mean my dad's cool and all, as far as dads go, and he *is* a musician, well a song writer now, but a punk band. Wow! That pretty much blew me away.

While I was in the midst of pondering over were-mom and punk-dad, apparently Aiden was more concerned about what soon-to-be-alpha meant. He turned to me with a look on his face that I didn't quite understand until he finally asked, "Wait. Alpha? What exactly does that mean?"

"Well, werewolves live in a pack. We're like real wolves in that respect. In every pack there is always an alpha, who is the leader," Mom explained.

"Are there a lot of us? I mean, how many werewolves are we talking about here?" Aiden asked, clearly as shocked I was about the whole thing.

"Oh, I don't know. I've been away from the pack for a long time. But yes, there are many different packs, and surely hundreds of werewolves here in America, probably thousands all over the world," Mom explained.

"So the alpha controls everything. Like the president?" Aiden asked.

"Well, yes, sort of. There are very specific rules when living with a pack, and if you're going to stay in the pack, then you have to follow the pack's rules."

Sounds more like a dictator than a president, but I didn't bother correcting anyone.

Mom looked over at Dad and smiled as she continued, "Being with your father was definitely not following the rules. And not long after we met, I decided that what I really wanted most was to be with him, but I couldn't, not without telling him the truth. I knew if we were going to be together, I would have to leave my family and the pack. There were very strict rules at the time, and I was breaking just about all of them. Late one night during one of our secret dates, I decided to come clean."

I looked over at Dad to find him smiling as if he was remembering that night.

"So this is where I can kind of relate to how you guys feel," Dad added. "It was quite a shock finding out that the woman you are in love with is a werewolf, especially when she just blurts it out. I'll never forget that moment. We were sitting on the floor in my dorm room, talking about nothing in particular, when she casually interrupts me and says, 'Would you still love me if I were a werewolf.' And well, after I came to terms with the fact that I wasn't going to be her dinner, I accepted it. I had to. I mean, what else was I supposed to do? I loved her, everything about her, even the fact that she could kill me with her bare hands… or paws, I guess I should say."

This was unbelievable. My mother, Lillian Wright, PTA board member, SUV driving, IT nerd was a werewolf. I watched Mom and Dad holding hands under the table and longingly staring into each other's eyes as if telling the story made them love each other that much more. On one hand, it kind of made me want to gag, but on the other, it was pretty amazing to think it all worked out, Mom telling him the truth and him not running the other way. I'm guessing not everyone would take that kind of information so well.

"So, without any plan at all, we ran off together and started a life here in Houston. I haven't talked to the pack, or my parents, for that matter, since the day I left. I miss them, but I can't say that I regret leaving. It was them or your dad and I made my decision and never looked back," Mom admitted.

"Wait, so we like have grandparents?" Aiden asked. "I always assumed they were dead and you just couldn't deal."

"Well, that's a whole other story. I told you both when y'all were little that your grandparents lived far, far away and then neither of you ever asked about them again, so I didn't mention it. Kind of worked out easy that way."

"Okay, not to butt in, but where exactly does this leave us? Me and Aiden, I mean," I asked, not sure whether I was ready for her answer or not.

"Well, let's see. All the stuff you've been experiencing is actually completely normal. Rapid growth, increased strength, and aggression. I'd assume your senses are better, like sight and smell, maybe even taste?"

"Is that why I'm freakin' hot all the time? I'm like having one long hot flash, like a menopausal old lady," I admitted, relieved to finally have a few questions answered.

"Actually, yes. Your body temperature is increasing. Werewolves are very warm-blooded. Don't worry, you get used to it after a while."

Aiden looked around confused. "Are you sure I'm a werewolf, Mom? I haven't noticed anything different about me."

"Really, Aiden? Come on! You've grown a foot in the last year, and you have girls chasing you down like kittens in heat. Thought I might have to take the water hose to 'em. Hate to burst your bubble son; you're a good lookin' kid and all, but there are these little things called pheromones, and they're bursting out of your pores," Dad added laughing to himself.

"Huh? Really? I thought it was my winning personality and these big guns," Aiden said, flexing his muscles like Mr. Olympia.

"Anyways, so what now, Mom?" I asked, rolling my eyes at my idiot brother.

"I'm not really sure. I mean, I grew up knowing I was a werewolf. I'm not sure how you two are going to be able to handle the change. Or even if you will be able to adjust to being a were in this setting. I heard of lots of weres who live outside of packs, but I'm not sure how it works with teenagers. It's something we will all have to discuss as things progress. But for now at least you know what's happening."

***

We wrapped dinner up with a whole lot of unanswered questions. Yes, I know what Mom is and what Aiden and I will be one day soon. But what about everything else? I got into bed and pulled the covers up over me. Then immediately threw them back off. I genuinely missed the days when I could snuggle up under the comforter to keep out the cold, but apparently, those days were long gone.

I closed my eyes hoping sleep would find me, but this was all too much to take in. There were so many questions I should have asked, but I didn't even know where to begin. *What now? What is going to happen to me? Will I be able to control it? What if I morph into a wolf in the middle of Calculus? Can that even happen? Will everyone keep hating me? Will I always be a freak?*

Chapter 4

ALLISON

It's my birthday today. Seventeen. I'm supposed to be excited, overjoyed, ecstatic, right? But what did I have to be happy about? That could be summed up in one word—nothing! I had no one to be happy with, except for my now totally dysfunctional family, complete with wolf mom, ex-punk-rocker dad, and the ever-popular brother, who couldn't wait to go out and party with his friends tonight after my oh-so-exciting birthday celebration.

After an excruciatingly long birthday dinner at Benihana's, Dad pulled into the driveway, and I couldn't wait to run upstairs and take a shower. I smelled like a hibachi grill, and with my new heightened senses, that wasn't a good thing. I had been resisting the urge to hold my nose all through dinner, and could barely keep my once-favorite restaurant's food down. Well, there's one more sucky thing to add to the list of sucky things about being a werewolf. I could no longer enjoy the one dinner I look forward to all year.

Of course, Mr. Perfect Werewolf, Aiden, gobbled up everything in sight like it was the best thing he ever tasted. According to him, he could smell it, but it didn't bother him enough to stop gorging himself. Jerk. Why did he have to be so good at everything? He was already a better werewolf than me, and we hadn't even become wolves yet.

While washing the stench of hibachi out of my hair, Aiden began pounding on the door to hurry me up. "I need in there, Al. The guys will be here any minute, and I need a shower too. You're not even going anywhere. Are you?"

"I'll be out in a minute. And no, I'm not. Thanks for rubbing it in," I shouted back.

"Well, maybe you should go out with me. You shouldn't stay home on your birthday."

I couldn't believe what I was hearing. He was only inviting me to join him because he felt sorry for me? Who was this guy? There was a time when he wouldn't have dreamed of going out without me on *my* birthday. But that was because he wanted me there. This invitation was clearly different.

I guess I shouldn't be mad at him; he still has friends, so I shouldn't blame him for not wanting to hang out with a social outcast.

I hurried out of the bathroom, trying to make it to my room without having to talk to Aiden, knowing it would only make me feel more pitiful. I had made it as far as my door when I heard him call out from his room, "Hey, if you're still up when I get home, let's sneak out front and have a beer. Like we did last year, okay?"

"Sure, if I'm up," I said feeling a little better that he was at least trying to be nice.

I plopped down in my papasan chair and tried to read a book, but for some reason, I was too jumpy to relax, or concentrate, for that matter. Attempting to ease the unexplained jitters, I instead decided to pace back and forth in my room. When that didn't help, I did a few jumping jacks. I even tried a mini makeover, but nothing would calm the anxious, itchy feeling inside me. It was the strangest feeling, and it didn't seem to be going away. What I really wanted to do was rip my skin off and throw it in the washing machine. Since that really wasn't a viable option, I grabbed my Adidas and headed for the treadmill. I had just showered, but at that point, I was willing to try anything.

I hopped on the treadmill and started out walking at a brisk pace, but that just wasn't doing it so I cranked it up a bit. I jogged for a few minutes, without any improvement, so I upped the speed even more. Before I knew it, I was full out sprinting. Never had I run that fast in all my life, and I wasn't even getting winded. After thirty minutes, I finally slowed it down and got off, completely flabbergasted that I had hardly broken a sweat. The good news was that the itching was gone, thank goodness, but I still felt uneasy.

I grabbed a bottle of water from the fridge, glad that Mom and Dad were nowhere to be found, and headed back to my room. Just as I closed my bedroom door, exhaustion took over, and I barely made it to my bed before I passed clean out.

"Pssssssst. Hey Al, wake up." Aiden was shaking my shoulders to rouse me awake. Not the best way to be awakened, by the way.

As I opened my eyes, I breathed in and immediately began to gag.

"Omigod, Ad! You reek. How much have you had to drink tonight?"

"A little more that I should have, but really I'm fine. Come on. You promised you'd have a beer with me. Let's go," Aiden said as he stumbled toward the door.

It was clear that Aiden was well above the legal limit, and he was lucky that Mom and Dad were already asleep because they would have to be complete morons to not realize that he was completely trashed. The last thing I wanted to do was sit outside with my wasted brother, but he was persistent. Before I got out of bed, I asked "You sure you haven't already had enough? You smell like a wine-o."

"I'm fine. Really. Now come on sis. Get your ass in gear. It's your birrrrthday," he slurred.

Not wanting to get into it with him at the moment, I reluctantly followed him downstairs and out to the front porch, only to find three of Aiden's friends waiting for us on the driveway. I pulled Aiden to a stop and pleaded to him with my eyes.

What was he thinking? Bringing these guys here, and Thomas of all people?

"Oh come on, sis. Loosen up. We're all friends here," he tried to assure me as he pulled me toward *his* friends.

"We used to be friends, Ad. Not so much anymore," I whispered more to myself than to Aiden.

Thomas smiled and winked at me as he tossed me a beer. "Yeah, come on, *sis*. We are all friends here. We could be really good friends if you're up for it," Thomas added.

Seriously?

I walked over and opened my beer, but made sure to keep my distance from the rest of the guys. Aiden held up his beer to make a toast and announced, "Happy Birthday, Al. To you being seventeen and to us being werewo—"

"Where we are right now," I cut in knowing it would make no sense, but had to stop Aiden from blowing our little family secret the day after we found out that we were soon-to-be werewolves. Could he be more of an idiot?

With Aiden doubled over in laughter, Thomas took the opportunity to grab me by the waist, pulling me against him. He whispered in my ear, "I know where I'd like to be right now. Between those hot thighs of yours."

As I shoved him away from me, I said, "Ugh! Not ever going to happen. Don't you think you have caused me enough trouble this week?"

"Come on, baby. You know you want me," Thomas slurred as he pulled me to him again, but this time instead of grabbing me by the waist, his creepy hand landed firmly on my ass.

Aiden clearly wasn't going to be any help, being that he was still cracking himself up. So I did the first thing that came to mind. Not only did I shove Thomas off of me once again, but this time, I poured my beer down his pants, and said, "Maybe this will help you cool off, asshole."

Before the can was empty, Thomas jumped back and shouted, "What the hell is your problem, you crazy bitch?" Then he turned to my brother and announced, "Hey Aiden, you need to get your sister in check, man."

Aiden pulled himself together, looked up, and shouted, "What the hell are you doing, Alli?"

"What? He grabbed my ass... again! This is totally your fault, Aiden. Why the hell did you bring him here? I told you he was a douche-bag." I barked as I headed for the front door.

"Don't be such a drama queen, Al. Christ! You don't just dump your beer down my friend's pants. What's wrong with you?" Aiden yelled.

That stopped me in my tracks. *What is wrong with me? What the hell is wrong with him?*

Just before I turned around to let Aiden have it, I caught sight of the light in the front room of our house flip on and knew either Mom or Dad was awake, but that little inconvenience did nothing to defuse my anger. Apparently, Thomas saw the light as well because he immediately said, "Come on guys, let's get out of here." And as the guys hurried to their car, Thomas turned to call out over his shoulder, "Later psycho!"

I watched them drive away before turning back to Aiden, "I can't believe that you would do that to me. What? Just because he is your friend I'm supposed to let him put his nasty hands on me? And you blame me?"

"Yeah, I kind of do. Lately, you blow everything out of proportion. Do you even realize how hard it is to defend you every day, especially when you do shit like that?" he admitted.

"Then don't. Don't defend me. I never asked you to. God, Aiden! You're being an even bigger asshole than Thomas," I said as tears started to sting my eyes. This was all I needed. Now, my one and only ally had turned against me too.

Aiden grabbed my arm as I turned to walk away from him, and when he did, something in me snapped. My vision narrowed and my pulse raced. Without a second thought, I lunged for my brother with everything I had. Before I had a moment to comprehend what was happening, I had knocked Aiden to the ground. Acting on pure instinct, I jumped on top of him and started punching, hitting, clawing, anything to cause him pain. To my surprise, he wasn't trying to restrain me. No, he was fighting back.

His fingernail raked across my cheek, but it didn't hurt. It just pissed me off more. He managed to flip us over, so that he was on top of me. He was trying to pin me down when my elbow made contact just above his eye. Blood. Lots and lots of blood poured from his face. There was so much, so fast, that it soaked my entire t-shirt. Seeing so much of his own blood must have stunned Aiden too, because he sat back and stopped fighting. All I could do was stare at what I had done to him.

"What in God's name is going on out here?" Mom yelled as she busted through the front door just a few minutes too late.

Immediately, Aiden slid off of me, and I backed away until he was out of my reach. Mom took one look at Aiden's face and rushed toward him. "Oh my God! Aiden are you okay?"

As my adrenaline slowed, I could fully feel the pain he had inflicted on me, and from the looks of Aiden, he was in just as much pain as I was, maybe more.

It was then that it hit me, what I had started, what I had done. I was so ashamed. I couldn't look at Ad. I couldn't look at Mom. All I could do was run to my room.

Chapter 5

ALLISON

I woke up the next morning face down on the end of my bed, with tear-streaked mascara dried to my face. I have to admit, I was a little disappointed that no one came to check up on me during the night. I mean, I did get into the biggest and most painful fight of my entire life last night. It certainly seemed worthy of some kind of attention. Even bad attention was better than nothing. At the very least, I expected Mom to either storm in my room accusing me of being insane, or come and get my side of the story. I bet someone checked on poor Aiden. God forbid I leave any permanent damage to his precious face.

After washing off the evidence of my pitiful cry-myself-to-sleep act, I wandered down stairs to fill my empty stomach, and found my brother sitting on the kitchen counter with a bag of frozen peas on his swollen eye. I was so not ready to deal with this yet. Without a word, I quickly snatched a Coke from the refrigerator, ignored eye-contact with Aiden completely, and hurried back up to my room. My muscles were achy and tired, and the scratch on my face was throbbing. Plus the anger that was only beginning to brew moments before was quickly mounting.

I couldn't believe Aiden. He should have stood up for me. He would have never let someone treat me like that a year ago. Apparently, this whole werewolf thing has turned Aiden into a complete jackass. It was like I didn't even know who he was anymore.

***

Just as I was about to dramatically slam my door shut I heard heavy footsteps coming up the stairs. It was Aiden. I would recognize those heavy footsteps anywhere. I gently pushed the door closed and hurried over to the window, sure that he was headed my way.

"Al, can I come in?" he said after a light tap on my door.

"Really Aiden, I'm not ready to talk."

"Come on Al. We need to talk, don't you think?"

This time I didn't answer. I wasn't sure if I wanted him to really go away or barge in to talk, with or without my approval. I turned to sit down on my bed figuring the old Aiden would come in, but, at the same time, wondering if this new were-Aiden would just turn and walk away.

He came in, just as I had secretly hoped.

"I know you don't want to talk, but I do, so I guess you'll just have to sit there and listen," Aiden ranted, and he tromped over to the other end of my bed.

I didn't comment, but decided to sit there and give him my attention, at least until he pissed me off again. As mad as I was at him, I didn't want to fight anymore.

He sat there for several seconds staring at the floor before he spoke. "Al, I really am sorry. I don't know what I was thinking. I never thought I had it in me to hurt you, and I just can't… I just can't believe I got that out of control."

He looked away as his eyes began to water, surely not wanting me to see him this way. Aiden doesn't cry, like ever. Not even when we had to put our dog, Greg, to sleep a few years back, and he loved that dog more than anything.

I was about to say something, though I wasn't really sure what, when Aiden continued, "I should have punched Thomas in the face. He's such an asshat. I shouldn't have let him get away with that shit. I don't know what I was thinking, Al. Really. I *was* smashed, but that is no excuse for what I did."

Before he could continue, I admitted, "I'm sorry too. I shouldn't have attacked you like that. I don't know what got into me. I was just so pissed off. I could have killed Thomas. He's lucky that light inside came on when it did."

Aiden laughed which, in turn, made me laugh. He reached over to slug me on the arm and said, "Yeah, he's one lucky son-of-a-bitch. How did you learn to fight like that, anyways?"

"Hell, I don't know. Lots of practice I guess. That makes four fights this year, you know."

Aiden looked at me, his expression suddenly becoming serious.

Uh-oh, I know that look. This can't be good.

After an extended moment of silence, Aiden finally said, "Last night, after I sobered up a little, Mom and I had a very interesting conversation."

"I'm sure. I mean it is not every day that your kids are trying to kill each other in the front yard. How pissed was she?" I asked, actually curious about how she took the whole thing since she hadn't bothered to come talk to me.

"Very, but that wasn't really what we talked about. Anyway, listen, she wants to be the one to tell you, okay. I just thought I should warn you. It's pretty heavy," he said.

"Just tell me, Ad. I can't take anymore drama this week."

"Alright, but don't shoot the messenger. We are probably going to be moving."

"What? Are you serious? To where?" I shouted.

"Don't freak until we talk to Mom, okay. Come on. Let's go find her and get this over with."

Just as we were about to walk out of my bedroom, Aiden turned to me and said, "And, hey Al… I think it's a good idea."

Before I could respond with *What the hell do you mean, a good idea?* he shot down the stairs and into the kitchen.

Mom was just hanging up the phone when I got there, and Aiden was already seated at the breakfast table ready for "the talk." We sure have been having a lot of those lately.

I took a seat next to Aiden just as he asked, "Who was that, Mom? It sounded serious."

"Actually, it was your grandmother."

And to that, Aiden and I gave a simultaneous, "What?!"

Mom couldn't seem to hide her smile. "My mother, your grandmother."

"Why were you talking to her?" I asked. I thought y'all didn't talk.

Just as mom opened her mouth to answer my question, Dad walked in the front door with the newspaper, a dozen donuts, and four venti Starbucks coffees.

"Hey! They live." He paused. "But look like hell," he added as he lightly ran his thumb over the cut on my cheek.

"My baby girl, your poor face. Looks like it hurts," Dad said before he kissed the top of my head.

"No, I'm fine Dad."

"Okay then, are we all getting ready for another Wright-family talk? I brought some serious-talk food," Dad said.

"I was just about to start without you, honey. I talked to Mother. She and Dad are planning a trip to Rome. Doesn't that sound fun? By the way, Mother says to tell you hello," Mom said smiling at Dad.

"No she didn't. Don't even try to butter me up," he immediately responded.

We all settled in at the table, and Aiden and I started in on the box of assorted donuts. There was definitely one perk to being a werewolf. I could eat all the donuts I wanted and not gain an ounce. Nothing better than a speedy metabolism.

Mom cleared her throat, preparing to begin her speech. "Kids, we're moving to Red Ridge, New Mexico. My hometown. And before you go all ballistic, the decision has already been made. I will *not* risk your safety, or the safety of others, for that matter," Mom said looking directly at me. "And I don't want to watch you suffer anymore, baby. You both need to be around other kids like yourselves. I went through my change a long time ago and things are different now. I'm not going to sugar-coat it; it's not an easy adjustment. It's going to be hard on all of us, but your father and I agree that it is necessary," Mom rambled on, hardly pausing to take a breath.

Aiden reached over and tapped my hand, "This really is a good idea, Al."

I couldn't help but roll my eyes at Aiden. How could he? Was he seriously trying to be consoling? Like I didn't already know that this was all my fault. That I was the one who couldn't handle the whole werewolf thing. Perfect little Aiden would probably handle everything, well… perfectly. It was me who was the big screw-up. Me, who everyone now hated. Me, who was going around kicking everybody's ass. No one needed to say it. I knew this was my fault. Did they really think that they could make it all better by uprooting the whole family to a new place? Did they really think this little move was going to fix all of my problems?

PART II

Allison, Kendall, and Cade

Chapter 6

ALLISON

The last two weeks flew by in a blur. When Mom announced that we were moving, I thought she meant eventually, not immediately. Both of my parents worked from home, so that made their decision a little easier, I guess. I barely had time to pack my room before Mom was shoving us in the car and we were driving away from Houston.

Surprisingly, Mom was patient enough to give Aiden time to say goodbye to his bazillion friends. Right before we headed out, a group of at least twenty people from school showed up at our house. Aiden's friends. Most of them used to be my friends too. They hugged him and cried, showering him with I'll miss you and keep in touch.

Hard to believe, but a few of them said goodbye to me too. Jackie Thompson told me to take care of myself, which was kind of nice, but it just wasn't the same. While Aiden said his last *see you laters*, I sat in the car wondering what that moment would have been like if it had happened six months ago. As we drove away, I half-smiled and waved to the group, but I knew in my heart that their waves weren't meant for me.

***

Looking out the window at the snow-peaked mountains in the distance, I found myself thinking about how good this move could actually be for me. I am going to meet girls that are like me. Surely, they won't hate me before getting to know me. Right? I might actually have friends again. I almost forgot what it was like to be able to call up a girlfriend to go shopping or to the movies. Or give someone a call when I needed someone to talk to about whatever the new drama was at the moment. Or even have good drama. The only drama in my life over the past few months was exactly what lead up to this move. Girls hating me, me kicking their asses, and Aiden being a shithead. I definitely needed new drama.

And guys… new guys would be good. So very, very good. I might even get a date with a guy who doesn't assume he's going to score within ten minutes of picking me up. Yes, this could be a great move.

Being off in my own little world, I was caught off guard when Aiden thumped me on my knuckles.

"What is up with you? Do you realize that you are smiling *and* humming? You look like an idiot," Aiden said, rolling his eyes.

I turned toward him, ready to reciprocate his insult, but the woe-is-me look on his face, stopped me. He was just sitting there, with glazed over eyes, and a frown that said more than any words possibly could have. I guess I was so caught up in my own new-found optimism, I didn't think about the fact that Aiden was probably having a hard time with all of this. I mean he actually had friends. He actually had a life that he was forced to up and leave on a moment's notice. He acted the whole time like this is a good thing, but I had to wonder how much of that was for my benefit.

Trying to lighten the mood, I responded, "What? I was humming? Really?"

"You know, I haven't seen you smile in a long time. Are you starting to believe that this might be a good thing?" Aiden asked.

"Of course not! I still can't believe Mom made us sell our car and is dragging us all out here to live on some freaky estate. It sounds kind of like a cult, if you ask me." I'm not sure why I couldn't admit my hopes were high. Maybe I was just scared of having them crushed.

Aiden didn't bother to respond, and instead went back to reading his book, but something told me he wasn't really reading it. He looked too lost in his own thoughts to just sit back and relax with a book, even a John Green book.

I reached over and tapped him on the knee. "Hey, you okay?"

"Sure, I'm good," he told me, but his eyes said the opposite. I didn't want to push Aiden into talking if he didn't want to. He could act like this is a great idea for all I cared. I knew the truth. If Mom and Dad would have made me leave League City six months ago, I would have been a disaster zone. There was a time when I actually had a life, and friends, and a boyfriend. I would have been devastated if I had to give all of that up, not to mention with only two weeks' notice.

Well, I guess I did have to give it all up not all that long ago. But that was different. They gave me up. Each and every one of them turned their back on me, and for what? Dad blames the pheromones, but I think it's just one of those questions that we will never know the answer to. Only one thing was for sure—my life completely changed in the blink of an eye, and I couldn't have been more ready to start over somewhere new, though I'd never admit it to anyone other than myself.

***

Just when I thought that my butt had suffered permanent and irreversible damage from sitting on it for too long, my mom jerked around and said the words that I had been dying to hear. "We're here!"

"Finally, I didn't think that I could drive for too much longer," Dad said with a small smile, but I could see the tension in his jaw when he turned to look at us. Poor Dad. It was going to be hard on him, being back here with Mom's family, and of course Mom's ex-fiancé, Marcus, who apparently is the leader of the pack.

Pack. We were going to be part of a pack. A werewolf pack. This was all too weird.

We pulled onto a long, narrow driveway that headed straight into a wooded area. If this was a scary movie, this would be the characters' first stupid mistake. There was just something eerie about the whole thing. Mom never mentioned that her pack lived in the woods. The deeper we drove into the brush, the more uneasy I became. The road winded around and back, and soon turned into a snow-covered dirt path.

"Uh Mom, why are we in the woods?"

"Oh Aiden, don't worry. We are almost there. It won't seem like the forest once we arrive. Y'all are going to love it. We are right on the lake." Mom paused for a moment to take it all in, and I wondered what it was like for her to be back after all this time.

"Are our grandparents going to be there?" I asked.

"No baby, they are still in Italy. When I told them when we were coming, my mother was devastated. Oh wait, let's see… Marcus said he'd meet us in front of our new home. Honey, it should be right up here on the left," Mom said as she pointed toward a clearing.

As we entered the estate, I could hardly believe my eyes. It was amazing. We might live in the woods, but we definitely weren't going to be roughing it. Our car pulled into the driveway of an enormous two-story house, complete with a huge wrap-around porch and two balconies facing a breathtaking lake.

Mom turned around just in time to catch Aiden and me with our mouths hanging open. "Isn't it beautiful? I knew y'all would love it. You know, all the houses face the lake, in a big circle. See?"

She pointed out to a huge community of homes encircling the water. All the houses were about the same in size but each had its own unique style. These homes looked custom built, not the cookie-cutter, suburban homes that have taken over every empty space in the Houston area.

Where did all of this money come from? These homes weren't cheap!

"How are we going to afford this?" I asked, still unable to believe what I was seeing.

"Oh honey, things are different here. This house, all of these houses belong to the pack. We all contribute in our own way, so as long as you're a part of the pack there are perks, and this just happens to be one of them."

At that statement, Aiden "perked" up. "Perks? Like what?"

"We'll talk about that later. Look, there is Marcus and Noel," Mom said, obviously disregarding Aiden's materialistic tendencies.

I looked over and once again my mouth hit the floor. *Omigod*, Mom's ex was hot, uber-hot, like Brad Pitt hot. Imagine the most gorgeous older man on the planet, and that was Marcus. Dad must have been one hell of a bass player. And his wife, Noel, was scary beautiful as well, and I mean it, both scary and beautiful.

As all the car doors simultaneously swung open, the frigid New Mexico wind rushed through the car sending chills throughout my unsuspecting body. My measly jacket just wasn't going to cut it living in the mountains. I wondered how long it would take to get used to living in a place this cold. I glanced over at Aiden and noticed him trying not to shiver, which made me feel a little better.

We piled out of the car and immediately Marcus came over to hug Mom, while the rest of us stood there politely smiling as we tried to appear that we weren't all about to freeze to death in our new sub-zero environment. It's weird that just a few days ago I was wearing shorts and flip-flops.

"Lily! It's so good to see you. It's been too long," Marcus said, while pulling Mom in a little too tightly for a welcome hug. Hearing Mom's little nickname, I looked at Aiden, and we both mouthed, *Lily*, at the same time. It would almost be funny if Dad didn't look like he was about to bust a vein.

"Noel, come over here and meet Lily," Marcus said.

This whole meet-and-greet was just too bizarre. So, I was extremely relieved when Marcus reached out and shook Dad's hand, and then handed him over the keys to our new house.

"Nice to finally meet you, Paul," Marcus said with his chest puffed out in true alpha-fashion.

"You too. Wow, this place is really great!" Dad pointed out politely as he surveyed the surroundings.

"Only the best for our Lily; she's been missed around here, you know. I'm just so sorry that your parents aren't here to greet you as well Lily. I'm sure they were quite disappointed when they found out that you all were arriving before they returned from their vacation."

I looked over at Mom, noticing the forced smile that was planted on her face trying to cover her anxiety. Still uncomfortable after all these years. Noel, on the other hand, looked completely unfazed by Mom's presence, like us being here was the most normal thing in the world. There was not an ounce of nervousness behind her deep brown eyes or her perfectly-glossed lips. Either she was confident in her standing as lead female, or she was one hell of an actress.

"So you must be Aiden," Marcus said as he shook my brother's hand. Aiden nodded and said, "Yes sir. It's nice to meet you." There was a look in Marcus's eyes that I couldn't explain, but it seemed that there was more he wanted to say to my brother but suddenly decided not to. He held eye contact with Aiden for just a second too long, before he finally turned his attention to me.

I was waiting for a hand shake as well, when Marcus took a step toward me and hugged me like we were old friends, "Allison, you look just like your mom did when she was your age, beautiful, just beautiful." It was a little weird and definitely unexpected, but friendly as well.

I was so relieved that these people seemed normal, kind of nice even. I was envisioning a bunch of hairy, vicious werewolves with too much testosterone.

After a few more minutes of chatting in the freezing cold, Marcus said, with a charm surely only the alpha could possess, "We are going to let you get settled. You let me know if you need anything… anything at all. And I am so sorry that you kids didn't get to meet my son, Cade, but I'm sure you'll run into him later tonight. And, Lily, your parents will be back in a few days. As I'm sure you know, they had that trip planned to Italy for months, but I'm sure they will swing by as soon as they return." And with that, Noel and Marcus turned and left.

Dad turned to Mom and said, "Well, after you," and we all entered our new home.

Excited to get out of the cold, I hurried in the front door to take a look around. The house was gorgeous. Gorgeous and huge. It must have been twice the size of our old house. The foyer opened up into an enormous two-story living room, and to the right was a kitchen made for a gourmet chef. The bottom floor also included a study and the master bedroom, but being that my main concern was my own room, I immediately headed upstairs to check out my new living conditions.

The stairs led to a game room, and on each side of the game room there was a small hallway with a bathroom and a bedroom, which were both the size of Mom and Dad's master bedroom back in League City. I could definitely start to like it here.

After settling in a bit in my own room, I went downstairs to help Mom unpack the boxes for the kitchen. I was organizing the pots and pans when Aiden came flying through the front door with his arms full of boxes. "Hey Al, I met some *teen wolves*," he said with a stupid laugh. "They invited us out to the lake tonight, you in?"

Of course, I was hesitant, but I decided that it was time to make a fresh start, so I said, "Sure, why the hell not."

Chapter 7

Allison

"Aiden, are you sure this outfit's okay?"

"Come on Alli. You look fine. It's gonna be great. You'll see," Aiden assured me.

Really, how could I be expected not to be nervous? It has been such a long time since I've been around new people. And these aren't even regular people. These are were-people. If only my stomach wasn't doing flip-flops. Surely, it's just nerves, but I literally felt like I could throw up at any moment. And if that wasn't enough, my heart was racing like I had just run a marathon. That can't be normal. Can it?

I stopped for a moment, just before we came into view of the others, so I could catch my breath. Maybe I just needed to sit down.

"What's wrong? You okay, Al?"

"I'm fine. I just don't feel very good. Come on. We're almost there," I said as I reluctantly began to move again.

"You're just nervous. You'll feel better once we meet everyone and you see how cool they are."

After a few more steps, a campfire came into view along with, let's see, six, seven, eight, nine, omigod, ten people. This was going to be weird, definitely uncomfortable, especially feeling the way I do. I stayed a few steps behind Aiden, letting him lead the way. As usual, he didn't mind.

Without a moment's hesitation, Aiden walked right up to the group and announced, "Hey guys. I'm Aiden, and this is my sister Al."

"Alli... hi, I'm Alli," I corrected him.

One of the older-looking guys jumped up and shook our hands. "Hey, I'm Sammy. And this, well this is everybody. Well, not everybody exactly. Cade and a few others aren't here, but let's see, this is Kendall, Cami, Shari, Misty, and Becca." Sammy went around and pointed out each of the girls and they in turn, gave Aiden a flirty little smile/wave combo, and surprisingly enough, they actually smiled at me too. I had almost forgotten what it felt like to be smiled at by someone other than my family.

"Oh thank God! Another girl. This pack is swimming with testosterone. No offense, Aiden," Kendall said as she walked over to stand next to me. She was oozing that overly friendly, yet fake façade, and some internal instinct told me to watch my back.

"And these are the guys: Ryder, Trenton, Tyson, and Luke. Now Luke here typically hangs out with the jackasses of the pack, but we tolerate him 'cause he's cool," Sammy said with a laugh as he shoved Luke's shoulder.

"Very funny Sammy. You better watch it or I'll tell Gage you've been talking shit," Luke responded, then looked my way giving me a playful smile.

All the guys stood up and shook both mine and Aiden's hand as they said hello.

Okay, first impression low-down...

Kendall must be the queen-bee of the group. She just had that air about her. I'd bet money that she says jump and all the girls jump without question. And she certainly looked the part: long, shiny, dark hair, chocolate-brown eyes with eyelashes that you could see from across the room, and the body of an Olympic athlete. On the surface, she seemed nice, but I couldn't shake the feeling that it wasn't genuine. And it didn't help that I could have sworn she glared at me before Sammy introduced her. Not to mention the fact that I noticed that Shari, Misty, and Becca all looked to Kendall for instructions, which apparently were *just smile and let me handle this*.

All of the guys seemed like really good guys, not the typical high school males that I had grown accustomed to back home. It was kind of a relief to finally have guys to talk to without worrying about them grabbing certain parts of my body without permission.

Glancing around the campfire at all of the new faces, one thing struck me as particularly odd. They were all extremely attractive. Don't get me wrong, some more than others, but all of them were ridiculously good-looking. I guess it's a were-thing. Who knows? But it did make me wonder if there was such a thing as an ugly werewolf.

The girls were all tall and athletic-looking, with long, dark hair. Kendall definitely held the title of most beautiful were-girl. I did find it odd that they all shared the same physical features, though none of them really looked alike. With blonde hair, light-green eyes, and all my new curves, I stood out like a sore thumb. *Great, I didn't even look the part.*

The guys could only be described as tall, dark, and dangerously handsome. They could totally be the next big boy-band. But with bigger muscles. Even the younger guys looked like they grew up in a gym. One word: gorgeous.

Finally, settled around the campfire, Sammy offered us both a beer. Still feeling a little light-headed and queasy, the last thing I wanted was alcohol, so I politely declined, but Aiden didn't think twice about opening one up and chugging.

Aiden fell into step immediately, telling stories and making everyone laugh. They all got a kick out of hearing about me and Aiden fighting in the front yard. He took it upon himself to get up and act out the whole embarrassing event. I sat there praying he wouldn't make me get up and participate. I think that even Kendall smiled—at him, not me—when Aiden admitted he got his ass kicked by a girl. I just kind of sat there and laughed when I was supposed to, but I didn't really join in the conversations.

Suddenly, Luke turned to me and asked, "So, you both really just found out you were werewolves? That's too weird."

I opened my mouth to speak when Becca jumped in and asked, "So, you two haven't changed yet?"

We both just shook our heads. "Should we have?" Aiden asked.

"We usually have our first change before we turn sixteen. But don't worry, Cami still hasn't changed and she turned sixteen... what two weeks ago?" Kendall said looking at Cami.

I felt bad for Cami. Kendall was obviously making fun of her.

"We were taught though. It will probably happen soon... for all of you," Luke said smiling at Cami.

Shari chimed in, "So, how could you not know that you were different? I mean, there are signs and stuff."

And again, before I could answer, Aiden interrupted, "No, not a clue. I just thought Al was one tough chick. Before she beat me up, she got her hands on three poor, defenseless girls at our old school."

"What? Really?" Cami turned to me for clarification.

And naturally, good ol' Aiden decided to answer for me. "Yep. My little sister here had quite a reputation at South Shore High. She punched first and asked questions later."

Before I could defend myself, Kendall found a way to cleverly take the subject off of us and turn the attention back to her. "So guess what guys? My mom said I'm getting a new car for Christmas. Well, technically, it's supposed to be for Christmas, but I convinced her to get it for me sooner. Anything I want. What should I ask for?"

With the focus being solely on Kendall and her important car decision, I leaned up against a boulder to try to relax. Though my initial anxiety about meeting the pack had passed, my stomach was still in knots, and I still couldn't seem to catch my breath.

I was nursing a beer that was forced upon me by Aiden when Sammy scooted over to sit beside me. "Alli, hey girl, you alright? You seem awfully quiet."

"Actually, I'm feeling a little off. I might just head home," I admitted.

"You want me to walk you?" Sammy offered.

"She'll be fine. Won't you Al?" Kendall said with a little pat on my shoulder, like she was concerned, but in truth, it seemed more like she couldn't wait to get rid of me.

"Kendall's right. I'll be fine," I told Sammy with as much of a smile as I could manage.

I walked over to where Aiden was chatting up some of the girls and told him that I was heading back home. He gave me an I-knew-you-would-flake look and then went to the cooler for another beer. I waved goodbye to everyone and headed back to our house.

Chapter 8

Kendall

Allison Wright… Allison Wright better watch her big-ass behind. There is only one queen in this pack and it is me. I bet she thinks she's so hot with all that blonde hair. Who does she think she is? Playing the shy-quiet-new-girl part. She may be tall, and tanned, and curvy, but she is still a nobody. And if I have anything to say about it, she will remain a nobody. There simply isn't room for anyone new, and I'm going to make damn sure that there is no place for her.

"Earth to Kendall. Do you read me Kendall?" Sammy shouted as he waved his hand back and forth in front of my face.

"What? Get your paw out of my face. I was just thinking."

"About what? Cade? Where is he anyway?" Shari asked.

Good question. Where was Cade? I didn't know how to answer that without admitting that Cade hadn't told me what he was up to tonight. We were supposed to be inseparable, supposed to tell each other everything, but the truth was that he's been acting weird all day, and things have just been, well… awkward.

"He had some stuff to do. And it's not really any of your business." I turned away from Shari and looked over at Aiden, who was laughing at something one of the guys must have said. Aiden was definitely hot, but not really my type. Being that I have been surrounded by weres my whole life, just another pretty face doesn't really do it for me. When he caught me staring, I ended up blurting out, "So Aiden, how are you liking it here?"

Aiden ran his hand through his hair before he answered, "It's okay so far. I mean, we just got here, so there's a lot to get used to, but I think I'm going to like it."

"I think you're going to like it too. You and my boyfriend, Cade, will probably be good friends. He's going to be our next alpha, you know."

Out of nowhere, Becca interrupts and says, "And Kendall here is just dying to get her hands on Cade's alpha ring."

I rolled my eyes at Becca, ignoring her jealous remark, and turned to talk to Aiden again. "You and Cade even kind of look alike," I said suddenly realizing just how true the statement really was. Cade and Aiden did kind of resemble each other, in a weird way. Maybe it's just their green eyes. Dark features were the norm in any pack, but every once in a while, you come across a were with light eyes. It was uncommon, but not nearly as rare as blonde hair, like Allison Wright's. Now that was something I had never seen. She probably thinks she's oh-so-special with her perfectly-golden locks.

I walked off to get another beer when I caught a scent of something unfamiliar in the air. My nose was leading me off toward the tree line when I heard Sammy's voice calling, "Hey, Kendall, what's up?"

"What are you? My mom? Just give me minute." I hoped he would think that I just needed to pee and leave me alone. I knew I didn't have to go far. The scent was getting stronger. After a few steps into the trees, I saw him. Piercing, blue eyes of a wolf I had never seen before peeked out from behind a huge boulder. Our eyes connected, but he didn't move and neither did I. We just stood there… staring. Whether this wolf was dangerous or not, I didn't know, but for some reason, I felt like I needed to find out.

Chapter 9

Allison

The further away I got from the campfire the worse I felt. At first, it came and went. A flash of nausea, a tightness in my chest, but now it was more like a tingly sensation all over my body. I swear I could actually feel the blood pumping through my veins. All I wanted to do was stop, lay down in the fetal position, and wait it out, but I needed to get to my house. I knew that if I made it home that I would at least be safely inside the confines of my room, so I pushed ahead with all the speed I could muster.

Despite the fact that I felt like I might faint at any moment, I was almost sprinting by the time I could see our front porch in the distance. Amazingly enough, the sight of it seemed to take the edge off my nausea.

I slowed to a walk and tried to catch my breath a bit. But that was when the serious pain started; I clutched my stomach and doubled over. Falling to my knees, I gasped for air. It was like, all at once, my heart had stopped, my lungs had failed, and something in my stomach was trying to claw its way out. I wanted to scream, but no sound would come. I rolled over on my side attempting to slow my ragged breathing, but the pain wouldn't let up.

I needed to get home. I lifted my head, pushed up with an arm that seemed to only be partially functioning and somehow made it to my knees.

After that, everything happened so suddenly. I wasn't even sure how. All I knew was that one second I was struggling to make it to my feet, and the next I was down on all fours… paws, that is.

Holy shit, shit, shit! This can't be happening. This-so-can't-be-happening! I thought to myself since I suddenly found myself unable to speak. I opened my mouth, well not my mouth exactly, more like my muzzle, but nothing but a low whine came out. With a little added effort, I forced out a pitiful excuse for a howl, and then quickly decided that practicing my howl wasn't the best idea, being that I could quite possibly attract unwanted visitors.

Looking around, everything appeared so different, so much more vivid, so much more alive. I could now see clear across the lake, the water shimmering from the moonlight, the fish swimming just beneath the surface, the dew forming on the grassy bank, the hundreds of insects encircling the nearby trees.

But what shocked me the most were the smells in the air. The rich soil, the thick grass, the lake water, each took on their own unique scent, and somehow I was now able to distinguish between them all at once. I had only thought I had a heightened sense of smell before. The scents in the air were comforting, like earth, nature, life… like home. It was as if I belonged; as if I had finally discovered where I was meant to be.

I found myself beginning to move, needing to explore, to follow the scents that were calling out to me. I took one step on my new legs, expecting it to be like learning to walk all over again, but it was nothing like that. With one step down, the rest followed with ease and before I realized it, I was running. In this form, on these strong legs, I possessed a grace that I have never known before. I was running as fast as I could through the thick forest, never missing a step, zigzagging through trees and brush, loving this new body and all that it could do.

I didn't know where I was going, but I didn't care. The freedom of dashing through the woods was all I needed. I finally felt comfortable in my own skin, which didn't make a lick of sense being that it was all so new to me.

I caught sight of something in my peripheral vision and almost laughed, or whatever the equivalent of laughing was in wolf form, when I realized it was my own tail swooshing along with the rhythm of my gait. I stopped to take a better look at myself. I was the color of honey. I kind of looked like my old neighbor's golden retriever, but way freakin' cooler.

As I stood there watching my tail swish back and forth, my thoughts suddenly drifted to Aiden, and I wished that he were here with me. That we could have made our first transformation together. He would so love this.

What he would look like as a wolf? Would he look like me?

Just as I was picturing the two of us racing through the woods together, I picked up on a scent that stopped all thought, all movement, leaving me standing completely still, breathing in a smell that I would never forget. A mix of earth, and musk, and honeysuckle, and sandalwood filled my senses leaving me with a need, a need to find this thing that was suddenly making me salivate, suddenly making me ache with desperation.

Without hesitation, my nose hit the ground as I began to track the enticing smell. I didn't look up. I didn't stop moving. I didn't stop to think about what I might find. None of it mattered. I needed to find the source of that wonderful scent.

In the near distance, I heard a rustling in the brush, which ceased the mission that had held me spellbound. I stopped dead in my tracks and looked around, spooked by what I might find, but what I saw was the last thing I expected.

Peering out from behind a tall oak, a wolf was watching me. We just stood still, staring at each other, neither of us moving a muscle. His amazing green eyes were in sharp contrast to his deep, dark fur. He was a much bigger wolf than me, strong and lean, and the glint in his eyes told me that he was no ordinary wolf.

I gathered up the courage to take one single step toward him and was surprised when he did the same. We continued this dance. I took a step, then he took a step, until we met in the middle near the edge of the lake. We stood with our noses only inches apart, just looking into each other's eyes. I couldn't stop myself from drinking in the intoxicating scent that he exuded. Somehow I knew that he was doing the same.

He took one more step forward making our noses tap together gently. If it was possible to smile in wolf form, I would have, and without the use of words, I was left with only one option. And I couldn't resist. Nuzzling his neck with my face felt like the right response. The need to touch him was so strong, but once I did it, I immediately felt self-conscious and backed away. He again took a step toward me and returned the affection.

Lightening the mood, the dark wolf hunched down as if he was about to pounce. This began a game of cat and mouse that seemed to last for hours. We chased each other through the forest and played like we were little kids.

I was running as fast as my new legs could carry me when I felt a nip at my hip that sent me crashing to the ground. Before I could regain my footing, the wolf was on top of me. He had me pinned down so that I was forced to stare into his brilliant green eyes. The emotions that flowed through me scared the living shit out of me, and I had to get away. I had to get away from this strange, dark wolf that awakened a need in me that I didn't know existed.

Before I could even begin to struggle, he leaned down and licked the tip of my nose, sending shivers from the tips of my new pointy ears to the tip of my new fluffy tail. I froze under his weight. He backed up just enough to let me regain my footing, and then he nuzzled my neck again. It just felt right, like we were meant to do this.

Seconds later, that familiar wave of nausea passed over me again and my muscles began to ache. I couldn't change back for the first time in front of this stranger, even with the connection that we so definitely shared. When I felt the excruciating pain start in my chest I panicked, and took off in the direction of my house, somehow knowing the way and having no choice but to leave my mysterious stranger behind.

***

I made it to the back patio just in time. The change was sudden, automatic, like my body just knew what to do. I couldn't have stopped it if I had tried. Unfortunately, my clothes did not miraculously appear beside me. This was a pesky little problem that I had not even considered. Freezing my butt off, I ran in through the mud room, thankful to find that Mom had already stocked a shelf with some towels and sheets. I wrapped myself up in a fluffy bath sheet and tip-toed through the house and up to my room. Still shaking from the cold, I ran to the window to draw the curtains shut. When I looked down into the night, I saw the dark wolf's eyes staring up at me from the shadows.

Chapter 10

Cade

Oh man. Allison Wright is going to get me in a lot of trouble, I thought as I stood and watched her change from a beautiful golden wolf to the most stunning woman I had ever laid eyes on, and I wasn't just saying that because she was completely naked. She was not like the girls from around here. She was lean and strong like them, but she had the soft, curvy shape of a human. But it wasn't her body that entranced me; it was her scent.

I could sense her; smell her since earlier in the day. I couldn't even go down to the bonfire for fear of how I might have reacted being so close to her. I thought I would be safe hiding in the woods. I couldn't help but find her. No one would blame me, right? I never dreamed she'd sniff me out in wolf form. I guess I didn't have to roll around on the ground with her, but she was just too hard to resist.

I stood outside and watched her window until her light went out; then I headed home... alone. On the way there, I concocted a plan: run home, speak to no one, and shower quickly before anyone found Allison's scent still lingering on me. As much as I hated the thought of her scent leaving my body, I couldn't risk someone finding out.

Unfortunately, it didn't work out like it was supposed to.

I could smell Kendall before I saw her sitting on the porch steps waiting for me. It was more than obvious that she had had a few drinks and was pissed off.

"So, I see you met her. You reek!" she said as she slithered toward me.

"Kendall..." I started, but she cut me off.

She moved closer until she was right up in my face and threatened, "You listen to me Cade Walker. You better stay away from her. I mean it. You really don't want to find out what I am capable of if you don't."

I stared at her in disbelief. The hostility in her voice was, quite frankly, a little scary. This was a side of her I had never seen. Well, I guess that's not technically true, but I had never been on the receiving end of one of her hissy-fits. It was obvious that she was serious, but still it surprised me that she actually expected me to obey. There was no way anyone, especially Kendall, was going to start telling me who I can and can't spend my time with.

I moved around her and put my hand on the doorknob and said, "Kendall, go home. I'm not in the mood to talk to you tonight."

With her arms now crossed over her chest, Kendall replied, "Excuse me? I'm not done yet."

"Yeah, but I am. Goodnight," and with that, I walked through the front door without looking back.

I was heading upstairs to wash away both the evidence of my new secret and the bad mood that Kendall put me in when my dad's voice interrupted me, "Cade, we need to talk. Now!"

I paused halfway up the stairs and took a deep breath. He was going to know. There was no way to hide the fact that I had been with Allison. If Kendall could smell her, there was absolutely no chance that the alpha would miss it.

Before I set one foot inside the study, my dad said, "You are not to see her again."

It was a command. There was no emotion in his voice, nor concern for how I felt about the situation.

I stared at him unsure of how to respond.

"Sit down, Cade. We need to talk."

I decided my best bet was to play dumb. "What's this about, Dad?"

From there, it truly was a one-sided conversation as Dad lectured while I listened.

Dad: The Wright girl is off limits. There will be no more interaction with her. There will be no more anything with her. Do you understand me?

There was no time to respond before he started in on me again.

Dad: You know your role in this pack. You will become the alpha, marry Kendall, have lots of pups, and lead this pack. I will not allow it to be any other way. Do you understand me?

Again, no time to respond.

Dad: I can't believe you would even consider, for one moment, that you would get away with this? What were you even thinking?

Dad: Do you even have anything to say for yourself?

Me: I…

Dad: You know what? Just get out of here. Go take a shower and wash her off of you before Kendall finds out and tries to kill you.

I turned to leave, not sure that anything I could say would matter anyway. But before I made it to the stairs, Dad had one more thing to say.

"And son, if I ever find out that you were with her again, you will be disobeying a direct order from your alpha, and I will handle it as such. And you know what that means."

Chapter 11

Allison

The overwhelming scent of bacon and fresh coffee woke me from my first disturbingly vivid werewolf dream. As I slept, my mind replayed the events of the night before: the running, the playing, the mysterious wolf with the amazing green eyes. The images burned into my memory of that night felt intimate, so personal that I couldn't even begin to imagine telling anyone about it, about *him*. And for some reason, about my change, too. I couldn't explain it. I didn't even want to tell Aiden that my were-side had made an unexpected appearance last night. At least, not yet. At least not until I find out the identity of the unidentified wolf.

The single fact that I changed into a freakin' wolf completely blew my mind. It was easy, natural, not at all like I imagined it would be. Well, it wasn't exactly easy and natural. Maybe that's not the best way to explain it, but even though painful at first, after it happened, I actually felt whole for the first time in years, maybe ever.

***

When I finally made my appearance downstairs, we all spent the morning unpacking, Aiden and I focusing first on our winter clothes, being that tomorrow would be our first day of school. We quickly discovered that we were in desperate need of something to wear so that we didn't get frostbite. Surviving in the Rockies during the winter would be quite a bit different than the winters in Houston that we were used to. In fact, different isn't really a strong enough word. In Houston, we would live in jeans and hoodies—not to mention the occasional shorts and flip-flops when a warm-front blew through—all winter, but here, I needed a damn parka if I had any hope of staying warm. No lie, a parka... maybe even with fur. How appropriate.

After an hour of searching through box after box of clothing and coming up with nothing, Aiden and I decided to make lists of all the stuff we needed from town, grabbed Mom and her credit card, and headed out in search of new wardrobes. We had some serious work to do before showing up at our new high school.

***

I was seriously hating life standing on our front porch freezing my butt off as Aiden and I waited for our ride to school. Our first day of school! And yes, we had to carpool. Carpool? Apparently, that's how they do things on the estate. We were being forced to carpool with the others because, and I'm quoting my mother here, "there's no reason to waste all that gas taking separate cars," which in my humble opinion is kind of sucky.

Seriously, I'm all for saving the earth, going green, and all that, but I'm seventeen. I want my own car! Who wouldn't? I wouldn't even mind sharing one with Aiden. So we all were going to have to sit down and have a nice Wright-family talk if our parents expect us to live here without our own car.

Watching Sammy's Suburban approach, I said a quick prayer that I wouldn't look too out of place in my new winter coat and boots. Never in my life did I imagine owning my own pair of boots like this. I wasn't even sure what to call them, but they were warm and you were supposed to wear them when it snowed, apparently. Aiden assured me that we wouldn't look stupid, but I knew my nerves would only die down after I saw what everyone else was wearing.

"Chill out, Al. Everything is going to be fine. You look great."

"Sure Aiden. Easy for you to say. Everyone already loves you. Like always," I said with a huff.

"It's different here, Al. I can feel it. You'll see."

I wanted to believe Aiden, but past experience was telling me to be cautious. We walked around the SUV, and Aiden opened the back door. There were only two seats left, one in the middle row and one in the back.

"I'll climb in the back," Aiden offered.

I looked up and saw the guy I would be sitting next to and froze. I mean literally froze. Forgot to breathe, forgot how to move my arms and legs, forgot everything except the color of his brilliant green eyes.

It wasn't just his eyes that had me hypnotized; he was smokin'-hot, absolutely-heart stoppingly-breathtakingly-beyond-gorgeous hot. Mr. Dream Wolf. With his shaggy dark hair and to-die-for olive-toned body, he could stop traffic in Houston. He made my wolfie-side want to sit up, pant, and lick his face.

"Hurry up, Allison. It's freezing. God, were you raised in a barn?" Kendall said from her seat next to *my* mystery wolf.

It was him. The wolf. Who was now human, obviously.

Does he know who I am? Of course he does. He saw me from the window. Shit, shit, shit.

Kendall's death-to-the-new-girl glare shook me out of my momentary state of shock, and thankfully my legs began to move again. Trying not to knock anyone in the head with my bag, I made my way over to my seat.

Aiden, who had already made himself comfortable, tapped the drool-worthy guy on his shoulder and said, "Hey man, we haven't met yet. I'm Aiden."

"Hey, I'm Cade," he said with a wave, and then he turned his attention to me.

"And you must be Allison?" Cade said as he held out his hand.

The second our hands met my insides turned to mush. It was as if electric currents were flowing through our finger tips, like static electricity.

"Yeah, I'm Alli," I said as I reluctantly pulled my hand away from his, which left me suddenly feeling empty.

As the car left our driveway, everyone began taking turns giving Aiden and I the run-down on our new school: what to do, where to go, who to talk to, and who not to. It didn't matter that we were all crammed in the car together with only inches separating each of us. It was impossible to hear, to pay attention to anyone, but *him*, and I hoped that no one was asking me questions that I wasn't hearing.

Needless to say, my concentration was shot. I couldn't focus on anything except the familiar scent radiating off the body next to mine.

Each time Cade moved, even the slightest shift, his spicy scent consumed me. I have dreamed of that smell for two nights in a row and having him near me now was teetering on being too much to handle.

How could I possibly feel this way? We only just met. I didn't even know his name up until a few minutes ago, but something inside me was telling me that none of that mattered.

The need to touch him, just to have some kind of contact with him, was almost painful. I wanted to cry, wanted to laugh, wanted his arms wrapped around me. I wanted him to nuzzle up against me again.

What the hell was wrong with me? Surely, he was feeling this too, right? Oh God! What if he wasn't?

I kept my eyes focused on the winding road ahead of us fearing that if I looked his way, he might sense what I was feeling, what I was thinking. No, I couldn't let that happen. I forced myself to keep at least an inch or so between our arms so that they wouldn't touch.

That is until Aiden opened his big mouth to ask how much further the school was. Cade turned his body toward me to answer him, and not only did his arm brush against mine, but I felt his warm breath brush across my face as he answered. He smelled of honeysuckle and brown sugar, and I had to fight the urge to grab his neck and pull his lips to mine. Lost in his scent and the closeness of his body, I wanted so badly to reach out to him just to feel that spark once more. The need was so strong I almost couldn't stop myself.

Just as I thought all control was lost, we pulled into the parking lot, and finally I was able to breathe again. I opened the car door, all but stumbled out, and sucked in the fresh air, hoping to ease the pain in my chest.

Cade followed me out, and as Kendall followed him she threw herself into his arms and whispered something in his ear. Kendall took Cade's hand and started toward the front entrance, leaving me walking behind the group.

Just as we reached the school's entrance, Cade looked over his shoulder at me. We just looked at each other. There was no smile, no frown, no expression at all. There were so many emotions running through me that I didn't know how to feel. Was I hurt? Disappointed? Angry? No, just lost.

Chapter 12

Kendall

I saw it. It was there. I would have to be blind, completely oblivious, not to notice the connection between Cade and Allison. If that little tramp thinks she is going to go and screw everything up, she's got another thing coming! It's not going to happen. Cade is mine. He has always been mine. I'll be damned if anything comes between me and that ring, or my position in this pack.

He will be the alpha male, and I will be the alpha female. Not some little half-breed whore. My mom would completely freak if she found out about this, and I guarantee Marcus and the elders would have a major problem if Cade up and fell for Lillian Wright's daughter, of all people. It's no secret that Lillian ran off with that human when she was promised to Marcus, which, in my opinion, should have been unforgivable. It was only because her parents are high-ranking elders that she was even allowed back after all these years.

At this point, there wasn't much I could do. I could alert Marcus, but I need to play my cards just right. So for now, I will have to pretend that I don't see it. Pretend it isn't there. But I *will* make it go away, one way or another.

When the bell for first period rang, I told Cade to walk me to my class. He gave me a half-hearted smile and followed me toward the west wing. I could tell that he didn't want to, but I also knew that he would do it regardless. Cade doesn't have the nerve to embarrass me in public. He knows better. When the halls were finally clear, I pulled him aside.

"Are we good?" I asked.

"Yeah... we're good," he replied, but his eyes refused to meet mine.

Just to be sure I had his attention, I ran my hand down his firm, flat stomach and whispered in his ear, "I really, really hope so."

He didn't move away or look around. He even moved a little closer and kissed me on the cheek before he left for class.

I know that things may not be normal between us, but at least I know that he's not completely lost to me.

If Allison knows what is good for her she will forget all about Cade Walker, and if she doesn't, that little bitch better be ready for a war.

Chapter 13

Allison

"Al, you okay?" Aiden asked as he turned around and waited for me to catch up.

I nodded and added a small smile, but I didn't really mean it. How in the world could I be okay? The guy that I was sure I was destined to be with just walked into the building with the supreme bitch of the universe on his arm.

"Come on, Sammy said the office is this way," Aiden said as he tugged lightly on my bag.

As we walked toward the office to get our schedules, the familiar stares, giggles, and ooh-la-la's followed in Aiden's wake. I swear he can't go anywhere without the crowd admiring his every step. Of course, Aiden was eating up the attention, giving little half-smiles and what's-up nods to the giggling girls.

"You totally suck." I couldn't help being irritated. Everything came so easily for him. I guess he could have said the same thing about me before everything fell apart a few months ago, but a little part of me secretly wished that he wasn't so damn perfect. It's just not fair.

"What? Don't be mad. I can't help it if girls are a little more obvious than guys," Aiden said in my ear, and as he did, I noticed three girls giving me dirty looks. That was all I needed; girls hating me because my own brother was talking to me. There was something totally wrong with this situation.

After a trip by the attendance office, I left Aiden to his own devices and headed to my first period, hoping to find at least one friendly face among the throng. I wandered into room 302 and looked around, not sure what to do when the teacher lumbered over and snatched my schedule out of my hand and announced, "Ah, Allison Wright. Welcome. Well don't just stand there. Go sit down."

Ms. Whoever ushered me over to an empty seat, and to my surprise, the girl sitting next to my new desk glanced my way and smiled. Stepping completely out of my comfort zone and hoping for the best, I held out my hand, and said as confidently as possible, "Hi. I'm Allison."

"I'm Teagan. It's nice to meet you, Allison" she responded.

Overjoyed to have someone acknowledge my existence, I smiled and said, "Nice to meet you too. I'm new... obviously."

"Well it sucks to be new. I should know. I just moved here last year."

I sat down at my desk, and after a few seconds of silence, I turned to Teagan to ask, "So, where did you move here from?"

"San Antonio. It's in Texas."

I could hardly contain my excitement. "Omigod! I'm from Houston, or League City, really. It's right outside of Houston closer to Galveston. How funny."

Teagan smiled a genuine smile this time, and I found myself hoping that I had found a real friend here, in this strange place.

"That is too weird. It's freakin' cold here, huh? I remember when we first got here, it took forever to get used to it. I bet you had to go buy those boots, didn't you?"

"Yes, I did actually. My brother and I had to go shopping yesterday. We had absolutely nothing to wear."

"I can relate. I had no idea what to expect when I got here. I was so worried about what everyone else would be wearing," Teagan admitted.

"Me too." I sat back at my desk, relieved to have made a connection here.

"Yeah well, I barely made it through the front door on my first day here when this horrible girl named Kendall made fun of my Wal-Mart snow boots."

"Kendall, huh? Maybe I should keep my distance from her," I replied, not wanting her to know that I was already well-acquainted with the horrible girl.

"So what else do I need to know about this place?" I asked.

"Well, let's see… this school is kind of crazy, but most people are really nice. I think you'll really like it, but let me be the first to warn you, because nobody bothered to warn me. There is this group of students here who act like they run the school, and well, they kind of do. But anyways, they are all crazy-beautiful, and from what I can tell, complete jerks. They only hang around with each other. And as you may have already guessed, the aforementioned Kendall is their lead mean-girl. Seriously, stay away from her at all costs if you can. You'll know who they are when you see them. I tried to be nice to one of them when I first got here, but she totally blew me off."

She gave me a once over and then shyly said, more to herself than to me, "But who knows, from the looks of you, maybe they will make an exception. You look like you just stepped off the runway."

For whatever reason, it didn't exactly sound like a compliment. I smiled, not sure how exactly to respond to that.

So my group of were-friends aren't so nice to the non-were people here at Carson High School. Interesting. Not that I was surprised that Kendall was a bitch, but I have to admit, I didn't take the rest of them for being such asshats, to quote my beloved brother. Maybe I should have listened to their what-to-do and what-not-to-do lists in the car, instead of thinking of ways to "accidently" brush up against Cade.

Looking at Teagan, she looks like she would fit right in with the pack. She's definitely pretty enough to hang with them, though she's shorter and curvier. But I guess the mere fact that she's human immediately made her an outcast. It's weird that they would only hang out with other weres. It made me wonder if they talk to any humans or if they strictly keep to themselves.

"So, you have a brother? Older or younger?" Teagan asked, knocking me out of my dazed and confused state.

"Oh… yeah I do. He's a senior, Aiden. I'm sure you will see him around. The girls are already throwing themselves at his feet. It's so annoying. So, what lunch do you have?"

"Third lunch, which kind of sucks because it's so late, and the group I was telling you about has that lunch. What about you?"

"Same," I replied, thrilled to hopefully have someone to eat with.

"I'll show you who I mean, even though I probably won't need to. They aren't hard to spot. I mean, if you want to sit with me at lunch, that is."

I smiled and gladly accepted her invitation. Entering the cafeteria was the part of the day that I was dreading most, and knowing Teagan would be there made the thought a little less terrifying.

Not long after the bell rang, Ms. Whoever began shushing the class so that she could take attendance and make announcements. She didn't bother to wait for everyone to get quiet before she began, but apparently, she had things under control being that it only took about five seconds for everyone to get seated, quiet, and attentive.

The entire class worked silently and diligently until the dismissal bell rang, and I might be completely pathetic in admitting this, but I really didn't want to leave Teagan's side. I secretly wished that she was in more of my classes, so I didn't have to be the new girl with no one to talk to, and she was genuinely nice to me. It has been a seriously long time since a girl was nice to me, genuine or otherwise.

On our way out of the classroom she told me to meet her in front of the cafeteria before lunch, and I silently thanked the good Lord above that I didn't have to wander into the scariest place on earth for a new student alone.

***

Before I knew it, it was almost time for lunch, and my morning classes weren't so bad. Nothing too exciting. Ryder was in my second period. I walked in and found an empty seat near the back, and when he entered the room, he walked right up to me and sat down like it was the most natural thing in the world. We made some small talk before the teacher began class, and he was actually really nice, not a jerk at all, but maybe, that was only because I'm not human.

Kendall's friend, Shari, was in my third period, and even though she was not all that friendly last Saturday night, she still waved me over when I walked in the room, like she had saved a seat just for me next to her, but then she hardly said three words to me, which, by the way, was awkward. I mean, just don't sit by me! All I could figure was that just because I'm part of the pack, she felt, I don't know... obligated? Too weird. I wondered if Kendall would have sat by me. God, please don't let me have her for any classes. Anyone but her.

The bell for lunch rang, and I followed the masses into the hallway. I found myself looking around for Cade. I couldn't help it. Obviously, he didn't seem all that interested in seeing me this morning, but I hadn't seen him all day, and for some stupid reason I felt like I needed to see him. Yes, I know. It's almost as pathetic as missing Teagan, my only new friend.

In my search for the one person I shouldn't be searching for, I saw Teagan coming my way, so I waved.

"Hey Allison. So, how was your morning?" she asked as we headed toward the cafeteria together.

"It was okay," was all I had the chance to say. because as soon as we walked in I immediately heard my name being shouted. It was Aiden and Sammy, waving me over to their table. The pack's table.

"You're friends with them?" Teagan asked, her eyebrows furrowed in a confused-disappointed-shocked combo.

"Not really. Well sort of. My brother is, I guess. Do you want to sit with us?" I asked hesitantly.

"Uh... I'm going to go with no. But thanks. It's okay. Really. I'll see ya later."

"Sure," was all I managed to say before Teagan high-tailed it toward the other side of the cafeteria. Bummed to see my new friend leave, I warily headed over to join the pack; definitely not sure if I would ever consider them as friends.

Before I could even sit my bag down at the table Kendall said, "Look who made a friend. That's sweet really, but just so you know, we don't usually mingle with the *domestics*, especially that freak. She seems a little damaged if you know what I mean."

Was the girl serious? Channeling my inner mean girl, I snapped back, "She doesn't seem damaged to me, but I'll keep that in mind, Kendall. You do realize that my dad is a *domestic*, right?" Not giving her the pleasure of waiting for a response, I chose a seat as far away from her as possible and then proceeded to dig in my bag for lunch money.

Seconds later, Cade, looking a bit stressed, dropped his backpack on the table near Kendall and let out a small huff. Kendall immediately stood behind him and started rubbing his shoulders. "What's wrong with my baby?" she cooed in his ear.

Gag!

"Nothing, I'm fine. Let's eat," he said as he shrugged out of her grip and got up to head to the serving line, leaving Kendall behind standing there looking quite disappointed. I looked around, noticing everyone else at the table suddenly wore the same expression, the what's-up-with-Cade face. And I had to hide my smile, thankful to not have to see Cade and Kendall hanging all over each other.

Chapter 14

Cade

I hurried off to the lunch line hoping that Kendall wouldn't follow me. I needed to be alone. It was killing me being near Allison. Being close enough to smell her was almost physically painful. I hadn't seen her all day, but I could smell her everywhere. This was not normal! How was I supposed to pretend like there's nothing there? There was definitely something there. Something I couldn't ignore. Something I definitely couldn't explain.

And Kendall. Somehow, I was supposed to be with Kendall even though the mere sight of her suddenly repulsed me. Where the hell does she get off telling me what to do? I totally get that she wouldn't want her boyfriend hanging out with another girl, but telling me that I have to stay away from Allison? Threatening to tell my father if I don't? How could I pretend that nothing has changed between us?

But, I had to. I wasn't exactly sure what my dad meant when he said, "And you know what that means," but I knew it couldn't be good. Would he keep me from being the next alpha? Kick me out of the pack? Disown me?

There was only one thing I could do. I didn't have the same options that others had. There were rules that I was expected to follow, no matter what. No one really gave a damn about what I wanted. It has always been, and will always be, *what's best for the pack* that matters.

Just as I was heading back toward the table, Sammy walked up and asked, "Hey man, you okay?"

I gave him as much of a smile as I could muster and lied, "Yeah, I'm fine. It's just a bad day."

Chapter 15

Allison

The only thing that I could think about the rest of the day was the possibility of getting to sit next to Cade again on the way home. The hands on the clock of the classroom wall could not move fast enough.

During eighth period, I watched the clock intently for the first fifteen minutes and then decided that by staring at the hands go tick, tick, tick, it was making the time go by slower. So I tried to avoid looking at the clock all together, but when I couldn't take it any longer, I looked back up, and it had only been four minutes. Then I proceeded to silently beg the time to move faster for the rest of the period. By the end of the class, I had taken absolutely no notes from the fifty-minute history lecture. Already off to a great start.

Yes, I knew Cade had a girlfriend. And no, he didn't seem interested in me at all today. He didn't even glance my way during lunch, though he didn't pay much attention to Kendall either. Who knows what he was thinking? It was probably not about me, but that didn't change the fact that my mind was on him. The worst part was that I was starting to believe that I would never be able to think of anything but him ever again.

So, imagine my disappointment when we piled into the Suburban after school without Cade. As we pulled out of the parking lot I saw Teagan standing near the curb, about to get in a friend's car. When she looked up, I waved. She saw me and smiled back, but didn't wave. This may just be a new record for me. Made a friend and lost a friend in seven hours flat. Now I had to endure the twenty-minute drive home without Cade.

Chapter 16

Cade

I avoided just about everyone all day, but Kendall managed to catch up with me before I made it outside to Sammy's car. Big surprise. I couldn't handle being "Cade" today. Not when the only thing I wanted was out of my reach. I saw Allison looking at me, even when I wasn't looking at her. I could feel it somehow. Her disappointment. Her confusion. What on earth could she be thinking?

Kendall tugged on my backpack strap to try to slow down my pace. "Hey babe. Can we talk for a minute?"

I stopped walking and took a deep breath, silently trying to convince myself that telling her to take a hike was not in my best interest. I needed, now more than ever, to play it cool. "Sammy's waiting for us. Can we talk when we get back to the estate?" I asked, wanting to avoid whatever it was she wanted to "talk" about.

"Actually, Shari said she'd wait for us and take us home."

Great, thanks to Shari this day keeps getting better and better.

"Okay, did you tell Sammy?" I asked.

"Of course, silly. Come on, let's take a walk." She smiled sweetly, but, somehow, I knew that sweetness was about to fade. She never stayed sweet for long when she wasn't getting her way.

We walked several feet away from the crowded front steps of the school before she stopped and faced me. When she didn't say anything I asked, "What's this about, Kendall?"

That was all it took. She began her rant, again, about how I need to keep my priorities in check. Number one, of course, being her. Here was how it went down:

Kendall: I want you to promise me that this whole little mess with that girl is over. I don't want to have to worry about what you are up to.

Me: It's over.

Kendall: Good, because I will not just stand by and watch you ruin what we have. And I will not share you. Are you hearing me?

Me: It's over, Kendall.

Kendall: I saw the way you looked at her in the car this morning, Cade. I'm not stupid. But, you're not either. I know you will do the right thing and stay away from her. You know Marcus will have your head if he finds out about this. And I would hate it if someone had to tell him what's been going on. You need to rethink your priorities. Keeping me happy should be at the top of the list. And you know what would make me happy, don't you Cade? That ring should be on my finger and you know it. Not to mention, if Marcus and Noel knew how you have been treating me, they would be more than a little pissed off.

Kendall was right. I had to stay away from Allison. And I would. Even if it killed me. Kendall and I were supposed to be together. And that was that. I would make this work. No matter what.

Though it was the last thing in the world I wanted to do, I pulled Kendall toward me and assured her, "Don't worry, baby. It's over. I mean it. I don't know what I was thinking. Really, let's just forget it ever happened."

And then I kissed her. Really kissed her. Hoping I could make her think I meant it.

Chapter 17

Allison

"Lillian, stop fussing with the couch pillows. The house looks great."

"I haven't seen my parents in almost twenty years, Paul. Can you blame me for being a bit nervous? Just go get the kids. Make sure they're dressed."

Aiden and I had been standing by the stairs for the last few minutes, not wanting to interrupt her panic attack. "We're right here, Mom, watching you freak out," I said.

Mom gave me a dirty look and then ushered us over to the couch, but warned us not to mess up the pillows. The introductions were about to commence. My grandparents were on their way over for dinner, and we were instructed to put on nice clothes, smile, and to be on our very best behavior. It was safe to say that Mom was thoroughly flipping out about the whole thing, but I couldn't blame Mom for being anxious. A lot had changed in her life since the last time they were together.

"I just heard their car pull up!" Mom said.

"You and your crazy hearing," Dad said. "Am I the only one around here who can't hear every little thing?"

Aiden patted Dad on the back and admitted, "No worries, big guy, I didn't hear it either." Then Aiden looked over at me. "Did you?" I smiled and shook my head. I had heard it, but I didn't want to hurt Aiden's ego.

Mom hurried over to the door to greet her parents. I expected lots of tears and hugs after all this time, but instead, it was handshakes and air-kisses. My grandmother stopped in the doorway and said, "Why Lillian, haven't you aged well?"

Mom gave her a smile and said, "Uh, thanks, Mother."

When they came inside, Dad was there waiting to greet them both with a handshake, and I wondered to myself whether or not Dad noticed how short they were with him. If he did, he didn't show it.

Our grandmother turned to us and said, "Well, this must be Allison and Aiden. Oh my goodness. I can't believe I'm just now meeting my teenage grandchildren." It was a stab at Mom, and I was quite certain that she didn't miss it. Irritation was written all over her face.

Our grandfather made his way over and said, "Let me take a look at you two. It's good to finally meet you both."

Aiden and I smiled just like we were supposed to and that was about it. No hugs. No affection whatsoever. It was like meeting your parents' co-workers or something. We all just kind of stood there in the foyer not sure what to do or say until Mom finally said, "Well, dinner is ready. Are we ready to eat?"

My grandparents were exactly as I had imagined them. Well... except I expected them to be nicer, more grandparenty. My grandmother, or Gram as she asked to be called, was tall and lean, and would probably be mistaken for my mom's very attractive older sister. My grandfather was tall, well-built, and had an edge to him that almost made him a little scary. He might be a grandpa, but I wouldn't want to meet him in a dark alley.

After a few minutes, we sat down to the most uncomfortable dinner imaginable.

"Well, everything looks delicious, baby," Dad said to break the silence, and to help ease Mom's nerves a bit.

My "Gram" scoffed at his comment. After that, we all dug in and started eating, and silence hung in the air like a dark cloud. Even Aiden, who always had something to say, remained quiet. But... in the middle of dessert, all hell broke loose.

"I just have to say this, Lillian," my Gram said. "I can't believe that you would leave your children in the dark about their heritage. What were you planning on doing when one of them transformed in the middle of the mall or something? I don't understand how you, of all people, could be so careless."

When Mom just sat there, obviously not knowing how to respond, Aiden cut in. "Really, Gram, I didn't notice anything." His attempt to get Mom off the hook only got him a glare from Grandfather, so he quickly shut up.

Then Gram continued, "Lillian, you should have known that you couldn't raise them in that environment. Teenagers can't be expected to just know what to do when the time comes for them to change."

Again, Mom didn't respond. Evidently, Grandfather didn't approve of her silence because he furrowed his brows and demanded, "Well, are you going to tell us what was going on in that head of yours, or are you just going to sit there and pout?"

Finally, Mom found her voice and replied, "Well honestly, I wasn't sure how it all would work out, but when I saw that things weren't going well, I called you and came back. That has to count for something, right?"

After another scoff from Gram, we all went back to eating our desserts in silence.

Immediately following dinner, my grandparents said their goodbyes. The door shut, and Mom just stood there, looking as if she was about to break down in tears. Knowing just how to handle the situation, Dad didn't miss a beat; he threw one arm around my shoulder and the other around Mom's and said, "Come on guys, my favorite show is about to start. Come watch it with me."

***

Unable to sit in the living room with the family any longer, I got up and excused myself from our *American Idol* viewing party when the show went to break. I couldn't concentrate, couldn't stop thinking about being back in the woods with the dark wolf. With Cade. It was a little unnerving to now know that it was Cade, who only a night ago was chasing me through the forest. Cade, who somehow seemed to know me, who somehow seemed to be connected with me, a connection I couldn't quite understand. But apparently, it wasn't meant to be. Now that I knew about a little pesky problem named Kendall Stuart.

I opened the refrigerator in search of something to occupy my hands, my stomach, my mind, but quickly decided that what I needed was not there. I grabbed my coat and boots from the mud room and called out, "Hey guys, I'm headed out for a walk. I need some air."

I didn't wait for a response before I closed the door behind me and headed toward the lake. It was freezing, but I didn't care. I couldn't bear to stay cooped up inside any longer.

If I had any idea how to become a wolf, I'd be on all fours already. Unfortunately, I'm not quite there in my werewolf training. Really, there should be a class or something, or at least a manual.

I kicked a few rocks on my way to the lake, watching them roll down the embankment toward the water that was attempting to freeze. As I breathed in and out, my breath made little clouds of smoke. Though my teeth chattered uncontrollably, I tried to embrace the frigid climate as I headed toward a pier that I had noticed last Saturday.

As the pier came into view, I quickened my pace. It was perfect. The perfect place to sit and relax, or in my case, to sit and dwell on the fact that even though Cade and I just felt right—in my mind at least—it seemed impossible.

At the end of the pier, the deck extended into an oversized gazebo with a beautiful patio swing. I made my way over to it, careful not to slip on the icy boards, and began to glide back and forth with my mind reeling about everything and nothing all at once.

If we had never moved, I'd be stuck in League City with no friends, certainly no boyfriend, and miserable. Instead, I'm here with one friend—sort of—and the most perfect guy that I can't have. I wasn't sure which was worse.

I swung back and forth, and back and forth, feeling more and more sorry for myself, as usual. There was a pity party a-brewing, and I was the guest of honor. Couldn't things just work out? Ever? Was that too much to ask?

What made this whole situation even more pathetic was that I only spent one evening with Cade, and I didn't even know it was him at the time. We didn't even speak, for Christ's sake! I should not be feeling this way about him. I needed to get a grip. It was absurd! But I couldn't help it. I thought about him constantly. I could still smell his scent in the air, and I was starting to fear that I always would. How was I supposed to get over this silly infatuation with my body betraying me? It was like I needed him, like oxygen.

My emotions were clearly on overdrive and reeling them back in seemed highly unlikely at that point. I closed my eyes as I felt a single warm tear cooling its way down my face. I was so caught up in my pity party that I didn't hear *him* approach.

I opened my tear-filled eyes to find Cade only a few feet away. He smiled sheepishly, walked around the swing, and sat on the other end, just far enough away that we didn't touch, but too close for his scent not to overwhelm me. Together, we swung back and forth in silence for what felt like hours, though I'm sure it was probably less than a minute.

"Allison, I don't know what to say," Cade finally admitted.

"Um, me neither," I answered honestly.

I held my breath as he scooted over. The closeness was agony but only because I wanted him even closer. He looked at me with those unbelievably emerald eyes, and my pulse surged. His dark hair was tousled like he'd been lying in bed, and his cheeks were flushed from the cold. I could feel the warmth of his presence through the freezing wind as he reached out and took my hand in his.

"I can't explain it to you, Allison. I don't know why, but I can't stop thinking about you," he whispered in my ear. I could still feel his breath on my neck long after he spoke. The sensation was both intimidating and intoxicating. I looked him in the eyes, planning to ask him about Kendall, but all thoughts were scattered as he covered my lips with his.

It took only about a millisecond for me to register just what was happening, and without hesitation, I pulled him closer to me and deepened our kiss. I didn't want it to ever stop. All I could feel was Cade, his warmth, his tenderness; it consumed me.

With his body pressed against mine, I drank in his scent, fighting the urge to rub myself against him so that his smell became my own. I never wanted anything more.

He pulled away leaving me breathless and placed his forehead against mine.

"Allison," he panted.

I couldn't seem to make my lips create words. I just stared at him, unable to believe what had just happened.

"I wanted to do that ever since the other night; when we met. I'm sorry. I probably should have waited; maybe said more than five words to you. I just couldn't help it, couldn't stop myself," Cade confessed.

"No, it's okay. Just kind of took me by surprise, you know."

With a coy smile, he replied, "Well, *you* kind of took me by surprise."

And before I could stop the words from coming out of my stupid mouth, I asked, "Cade, what are we doing? What about Kendall?" She was the last person I wanted to think about, but being that I just made out with her boyfriend, I had enough sense left to know that some clarification was in order.

"You're right. I shouldn't have kissed you like that. But... there is something between us. I feel it. I know you feel it too. Right?"

Was he crazy? Of course, I felt it too. I wanted nothing more than for him to kiss me again and preferably not stop this time.

I pulled back slightly and asked, "So what now?" I wanted him to tell me that he would end it with Kendall. That he wanted me, not her. That we were meant to be, and Kendall would just have to deal with it. But that was not what he said.

With confusion in his eyes, he said, "I don't know. I'm not sure what to do. It's complicated. Kendall and I..."

My defenses kicked in, and suddenly I didn't want to hear his excuses. "You don't have to explain. I get it. Really," I said even though I didn't. I didn't want to sit there and listen to why he and Kendall were "complicated." What did he expect me to do? Beg him to break up with her?

I started to get up, but Cade pulled my hand back down. "Just give me some time. We'll figure this out." And before I knew it, his lips met mine again.

Chapter 18

Kendall

That son-of-a-bitch! I'll kill him, but not before he is painfully neutered.

Hidden in the brush, I couldn't believe what I was seeing. I trudged all the way down here just to find him, so I could be all oh-I-want-you baby, and instead, I find him with that slut-puppy!

I stood there, unable to tear my eyes away from Cade and Allison practically making it on the dock.

He couldn't get away with this! I started to run over there and confront the lip-locked losers when a strange, yet vaguely familiar scent wafted through the air. Not sure who or what the smell belonged to, I turned my attention to it instead. I didn't think the cheating scumbags were going anywhere anytime soon, and I always trusted my gut, which was now screaming *go find whatever's out there*. While my human nose could not pick up the exact location of the scent, I knew exactly how to find the source.

Not wanting to be seen or heard by Cade, I snuck away deeper into the woods. Quickly, I stripped off my clothes and changed into my wolf form. Immediately, I picked up the scent and followed it. It was coming from just the other side of the lake, and it didn't take me long to find those same piercing blue eyes from before.

The last time I saw him, he was able to get away. I had only taken a few steps toward him when he disappeared into the brush. With my nose to the ground, I had dashed toward the area in which he had vanished, but he was long gone. I wouldn't let that happen a second time. I didn't know who this wolf was, but it was about time I found out.

Our eyes met and immediately my pulse began to race. He was new. No one I ever met before. Even if I had seen him as a human, I would have known.

He just stood there, staring at me. For some reason, I couldn't move. My wolf legs stiffened, and I was… scared?

I don't get scared? Do I?

Something about him was completely freaking me out, and I didn't like it. We continued our staring contest for a few minutes, but before I could stop myself, my eyes shifted away.

When I looked back up, he was gone.

Damn-it!

***

I stood there completely dumbfounded. Cade was making out on the pier with Allison-freakin'-Wright, some mysterious wolf seemed to be stalking me, and I was standing in the middle of the woods without a clue as to what to do now.

I backtracked to where I had left my clothes, shed my wolfy form, and quickly got dressed. One glance toward the pier told me that Cade and Allison had taken their little romantic encounter elsewhere, so it appeared that my only option was to head back home and figure out what the hell to do.

I opened the front door only to find my mother, with a half-empty wine glass in her hand, waiting for me. She turned off the television, refilled her glass, and asked, "So what's up with you and Cade? And don't lie to me. Something is going on."

"Hello to you too, Mother," I replied after shutting the front door.

"Something's up. I can tell. I saw him earlier today, and he could hardly look at me. And where has he been? Obviously, not with you. I would be able to smell him."

I dropped my purse on the console table and made my way toward the stairs.

"I want an answer, Kendall!"

"Well, I don't have one for you, Mom. But don't worry. Things will be back to normal before you know it." I disappeared up the stairs, but not before I heard her say, "They better be."

Chapter 19

Cade

I wasn't sure what the hell I was doing. I was even less sure about how Kendall would react when I told her that we needed to take a break. Take a break. That's what I planned to call it. I can't exactly "break up" with her. Not when my father has forbidden me to see Allison. Somehow, I needed to convince Kendall to still "pretend" to be my girlfriend. What was I thinking? I had no clue what I was doing.

I headed over to Kendall's early, way before Sammy would arrive to pick us up. I texted and told him that I was going to drive Kendall to school. I figured that she could just take her own car, if she refused to ride with me after what I had to say.

I wasn't sure whether or not to knock on her door, so I texted her, and told her that I was waiting outside.

After a ten-minute wait, she threw open the door, pulled me inside, and said, "What the hell are you doing here?"

"Uh, good morning to you too," I said, attempting to make light of the situation. "Is your mom up?"

Rolling her eyes, she admitted, "No, she's sleeping off another hangover."

That immediately made me feel even worse about what I was going to tell her. Kendall's mom did a good job appearing to be a totally-together member of the pack on the outside, but behind closed-doors, it was a whole other story, and only I was privy to this information. Even Shari didn't know that Kendall's mom couldn't go to bed at night without at least a few glasses of wine.

Not sure what else to say, I asked, "Can we sit down?"

We moved over to the couch, and Kendall didn't waste any time. "Don't think I don't know what this is about. I saw you with Allison. Don't try to play me for a fool, Cade."

Shit! I wasn't expecting that. "That was a mistake, Kendall. Look, I'm not sure what to do, but Allison and I are not an option. Don't think I don't know what would happen if my dad found out about that, not to mention the elders."

"Have you completely lost your mind, Cade? How could you do this to me? How am I supposed to react, knowing that you've been off messing around with another girl? We are supposed to be together," she whined.

Her attempt to make me feel bad for her was almost humorous. I mean, I should feel bad, but I knew that this was more about her and what people would think, than it was about our relationship. Plus, I could tell she was trying to produce some tears to go along with her plea to try to make me feel worse, but it wasn't working because she never cries. Never.

"I'm sorry, Kendall. I really am. I'm not sure what to say. I know it was wrong. But I need to be honest with you."

She cut me off. No big surprise there.

"Oh, you need to be honest? Seriously?"

"Yes, I'm trying to be honest here. I'm trying to do the right thing. I need a break. I need some time to figure things out. I…I don't know what to do here. I'm not with Allison. I'm not going to be with Allison. I just can't be with you either right now."

Her jaw dropped to the floor. She stood up, and the look in her eyes told me that she was trying not to brutally attack me. "So, what? You are breaking up with me?"

I stood up too, just so that she wasn't standing over me. "Not exactly. I know what would happen if my dad found out that we broke up. Can we just keep this between us? Really, Kendall. I just need some time to think."

"Are you really asking me if I will pretend we are still together when you are clearly breaking up with me? Do you know how crazy you sound?"

She was right. I did sound crazy, but I didn't know what other option I had. Some Walker charm was clearly in order. I grabbed her hand and pulled her into a hug. "I really want us to work. I just need some time to figure out what's going on with me. Trust me, I don't want to mess up what we have. Just give me some time. Please, baby?"

Kendall pulled away and looked me straight in the eye. "Fine! I'll give you your time. I'll even pretend that everything is just peachy, but don't fuck me over, Cade. I mean it. And you better stay away from that girl."

I had what I needed. Time. Time to figure this whole thing out. Now I just needed to make sure my father didn't suspect anything.

With my mission accomplished, I smiled and said, "Can I drive you to school?"

Chapter 20

Allison

On the way to school, I got a text from Cade asking me to meet him before first period. He wasn't in Sammy's car, and when Kendall wasn't either, I didn't know what to think. I met Cade at the side of the school, but we only had a few minutes before the tardy bell rang.

He pulled me into a doorway as if he didn't want anyone to see us together.

"Hey," Cade said sounding a bit out of breath.

"Hey, yourself."

Cade looked around, confirming my suspicion that he didn't want to be seen with me.

"Can we meet tonight? I need to see you," he asked.

"What? Where?"

"Can you sneak out? I can meet you down the street, and we can get off of the estate for a bit."

"What's going on here, Cade?"

The bell rang, and we both needed to get to class. He took my hands into his and pleaded, "Just say you'll meet me. I'll text you. Just be ready at around eleven. And ignore everything you see today. I'm not with Kendall. I'll explain everything tonight. I promise."

And before I could respond, he kissed me. Hard on the lips, and then took off for the gym.

***

After completely avoiding all things furry for the rest of the school day, I counted down the hours until it would be time to make my grand escape. Aiden never went to bed before midnight, so I decided it would be best to take my chances with the tree outside my window.

Right past eleven, I received a cryptic message from Cade telling me where to meet him. I opened the window, said a prayer, and proceeded to make my way down, hoping that the wolf in me would somehow make me a pro at scaling my way down a tree. By the grace of God, I made it down in one piece and followed the dirt road not far from my house, as instructed. And just like he said, Cade was waiting for me next to a motorcycle.

I could hardly contain the butterflies swarming in my stomach as I said, "So, where to?"

Cade handed me his spare helmet and simply replied, "Hop on."

I ignored my conscience, screaming that this wasn't a good idea, and instead wrapped my arms around him. Before I could decide otherwise, we were off into the night.

Chapter 21

Cade

There was no easy way to convince Allison to go along with my plan. All I could do was ask her. I headed toward a park that I knew of that wasn't too far from the estate, but far enough away that we wouldn't be seen. It was freezing, and I knew we wouldn't be able to stay out too long, but the park had an enclosed gazebo-type thing that would at least keep the wind out.

When we arrived, I parked my bike, and I took Allison's hand. I led her over to a bench, just waiting for her to ask me what was going on. Surprisingly, she didn't. Instead, we made it all the way there and sat down, but the look in her eyes told me that she was more than ready for an explanation.

I sat facing her and finally decided to just say it. "Allison, I'm not sure how to say this. And I'm even less sure what you are going to think."

"Cade, just say it. Just say something. What is going on in that head of yours?"

All I wanted to do was kiss the living daylights out of her, which made it even more difficult to figure out just how to tell her what I needed to say. "Okay, I told you before that things were complicated between Kendall and me. The thing is, things work differently within our pack. And it's no secret that I will be alpha one day in the near future. And well, Kendall... Kendall is supposed to be the alpha-female. I know it sounds completely crazy, but Kendall and I have been together for a long time, and it's just, I don't know... expected that she will be my mate."

The semi-hopeful look on Allison's face disappeared as she asked, "So, what are you telling me, Cade? I mean, if you are supposed to be with Kendall, then why are we sitting here now... together?"

I moved a bit closer, took her hand, and slid my fingers between hers. "Because I want to be with you."

"Then be with me," she said staring down at our intertwined hands.

"It's not that easy. Look, I talked to Kendall today and told her that I needed to take a break. I don't want to be with her, but I need some time. My father and the pack elders will freak out if I break up with Kendall and start going out with you. I know it sounds nuts, but I can't do that."

She pulled her hand away and my heart sank. She wasn't going for it. Why did I think for one second that this could work?

"I still have no idea what you are trying to say, Cade?"

"I have to pretend to be with Kendall, just pretend. Until I figure out what to do. Kendall and I are not together. I told her today. Please, Alli, say something."

"I don't know what to say."

Having no idea what else to say either, I did the only thing I could think to do. I wrapped my arms around her and did the one thing that I wanted to do since I saw her walking down that dirt path. I kissed her.

And she kissed me back.

Chapter 22

Allison

Three fabulous weeks. For three weeks, I have been sneaking out of my house, night after night, to be with Cade, and to be honest, these have been the best three weeks of my entire life. He's so amazing, but… yes, of course, there's a but. He does have one major flaw. He has a girlfriend. A girlfriend who doesn't seem to be going away. Major flaw!

Yes, Kendall and Cade were still technically together, which obviously sucked, and even though Cade promised me that it was only a façade to keep the pack elders happy, I couldn't help but ask myself every five minutes or so what the hell was I thinking.

But here I was again. It was Saturday night, and I was getting ready to sneak out. It was like I had no willpower, no self-control around him. I knew in my head that my relationship with Cade was wrong in more ways than one, but I couldn't stop my heart from wanting it to continue. I wanted to see him. I wanted to be with him. So I kept on going back, despite the fact that everyone, including my entire family, thought that Kendall and Cade were still together.

Taking one more look in the mirror at my guilt-ridden face, I grabbed my bag, filled it with the change of clothes that Cade said to bring with me, and headed out my window. Maybe we're going to the hot springs… again.

We went to five movies, three trips to the hot springs, and a few stops at the all-night coffee shop on the outskirts of town, all in hopes of avoiding other members of the pack. Secret dating was getting more than a little old. We were running out of places to go, but at least Cade was trying to keep things interesting.

Thank God I'm not afraid of heights. Sneaking out of a two-story house was no easy task. Climbing up and down the tree the first few times was a little tricky, but it wasn't long before I was pretty good at it. We had our routine down pat. Cade waits for me just down the dirt road from my house by a huge oak tree that keeps him semi-covered. He always looks uber-hot leaning up against his motorcycle in his leather jacket and jeans, very James Dean. Tonight was no exception.

"Hey angel," Cade said as he walked toward me.

"Hey yourself," I responded coyly, knowing that my favorite part of the night was about to commence.

After an entire day of acting like there was nothing going on between us, I could hardly wait for his lips to meet mine. I hurried toward him and wrapped my arms around his neck. His soft lips melded into mine, he took his time, like he wanted to memorize every inch of my mouth, and I immediately turned to goo.

When our lips finally parted, Cade grabbed my bag and handed me my helmet.

"Where are we going? The hot springs?" I asked, trying to sound excited, but secretly hoping we would do something new.

"No, I have a surprise for you."

A smile spread across my face as I hopped on the back of his motorcycle, wrapped my arms around him, and buried my face in his scent. Now that I had Cade back in my arms, I wouldn't have minded if we just rode around all night on his bike. If only it wasn't so freakin' cold.

We didn't drive far, and we never left the estate, so I was a little surprised when he stopped his bike and helped me off.

"It's my dad's old hunting lodge," Cade said as he pointed toward the front porch.

"Will anyone catch us here?" I asked.

"He hasn't used it in years, so unless someone followed us here, no."

Cade unlocked and opened the front door. He took out a flashlight and led the way inside. It was almost as cold inside as it was outside. Seeing me shiver, Cade hurried over to the fireplace to get a fire going.

"So, why are we here?" I asked, thinking to myself that there was really only one reason for a guy to take a girl to an abandoned hunting lodge in the middle of the night, and Cade and I were not quite there yet. Technically, we weren't even a couple.

As if reading my mind, he replied, "It's not what you're thinking, Alli. I really do have a surprise for you."

"Okay, so out with it," I said, immediately blushing.

"What did you want me to help you with?" he asked.

"Really? You mean it?"

I had been bugging the hell out of Cade to teach me how to manage my transformation. I wanted to learn how to turn into a wolf whenever I choose, and not just when I couldn't help it. Since I had no idea how to control it, I needed someone to help me. Was that too much to ask? Obviously, it wasn't on my mom's to-do list.

"You ready to figure this thing out?" Cade asked as he motioned for me to stand in front of him.

"I'm ready! What do I do first?" I asked.

Cade put his arms around me and whispered in my ear, "Relax and concentrate on changing. Clear your mind of everything else. Imagine yourself as a wolf."

He pulled away so that we were facing each other, and I couldn't help but giggle.

"Seriously! Stop laughing. Maybe it will help to sit," he suggested.

I sat down by the fire and tried to meditate, to relax my muscles, slow my breathing, and picture myself running through the woods with Cade by my side. Though I could picture the image clearly in my mind, after a few minutes I decided that this method was crap and definitely not working. Maybe I'm not the meditating kind of girl, not to mention, I felt like a complete idiot knowing that Cade was sitting there staring at me.

"It's not working," I complained in my poor-pitiful-me voice.

"Just give it a minute. Close your eyes. Imagine the tightness in your chest, the smell of the earth under your paws, the wind flowing through your thick, blonde fur."

I really tried to be serious, but "the wind through my fur…" Come on! Is he for real?

Before I knew it, another giggle escaped, which quickly became all out laughter. It wasn't long before Cade joined in and agreed that meditation wasn't going to work.

Our laughter finally subsided and Cade said, "Okay, so let's try this. I'm going to make you really mad."

I gave him my most seductive smile, rubbed his arm gently, and teased, "Oh, Cade. You couldn't make me mad. No matter how hard you tried."

Before he could respond, I trailed little kisses along his neck to tease him.

Just as my lips made their way back up to his, he responded, "Well there is one other way to try to bring on the change." With that, Cade pressed his lips to mine. This kiss was strong and dominating, he turned me around so that my back was up against his chest, and began kissing the back of my neck and shoulders. I felt a flood of heat spreading throughout my entire body.

"Close your eyes, Allison," Cade whispered in my ear.

"Imagine me chasing you through the woods. Imagine me nipping at your hind legs," Cade said as his kisses gained intensity, and chills spread over my arms.

"Imagine what would happen if I caught you, and I will catch you, Allison."

Well that did it. Instantly, I felt the familiar feeling of my impending change, but this time, it was different. With this change, there was no pain. No doubling-over, no clinching, no aching muscles. None whatsoever. It was fluid, like it was supposed to be. It was immediate. It was perfect.

So now what? I'm on all fours and Cade is sitting there cross-legged looking all smug, like he just won the Super Bowl. I pranced up to him and gave him a little lick on the nose, and then jerked my head toward the door, wanting him to hurry the heck up and change too. I was ready to play. I wanted to run.

"I'm coming. Hold your horses and give a guy some privacy, would ya?" Cade said as he motioned for me to turn around with his finger.

I knew he was stripping his clothes off so they wouldn't get shredded to bits, and I really tried not to look, but I couldn't resist. I peeked over my shoulder and caught a glimpse of the backside of one very naked Cade Walker. Before I could stop myself, a tiny little growl escaped my muzzle, and I immediately turned back around as he shouted, "Hey! No peeking!"

Seconds later, a giant, dark wolf was at my side pushing open the door with his nose. Good thing he was smart enough not to close it all the way. Guess you learn a thing or two when you spend enough time in this form.

Cade stepped out of the way to let me out, and the chase was on.

Chapter 23

Cade

What the hell? I was sure that I had left my window open when I snuck out to meet Allison. I have been sneaking out almost every night, and a locked window could only mean one thing. My dad knew. Avoiding my father for the past three weeks has been like a full-time job, but now there was no way around it. I would have to face him.

What I wanted more than anything was to stand up to my dad and tell him that Kendall and I were over for good. While we may have kept up appearances at pack functions and school, our relationship was over, as far as I was concerned.

On one hand, I felt like a complete jerk asking Kendall to play along, but on the other, I knew the true reason she was doing it, and it wasn't because of her feelings for me. The only reason Kendall agreed to our little charade was to maintain her status in the pack, but honestly, I think in her crazy-ass mind, she truly believes that at some point I will beg her to take me back. Kendall resides in her own little my-life-is-perfect bubble, and she would freak if anyone found out that things weren't as perfect as they appeared.

I took my time walking around to the front of the house knowing that Dad would be waiting for me. I wasn't kidding myself. This wasn't going to go well. It kind of felt like I was a convict headed into prison for his first day on the inside.

As soon as I walked in the door Dad grabbed me by the shoulders and threw me up against the wall. As he stormed toward me, he shouted, "I gave you an order, Cade. A direct order; and you disobeyed me."

His hands gripped the collar of my shirt, holding me up against the wall. My toes barely grazed the ground.

"You will not see her again!" he growled as he tossed me to the floor like I weighed next to nothing.

Never had my father been violent. Never had I seen this side of him. The fury in his eyes overwhelmed me, and I felt true fear for the first time in my life.

I remained on the ground but looked up at him to admit, "I'm sorry, Dad. I can't. I can't stay away from her. I tried. I really did. You don't understand."

He backed away, suddenly appearing calm, composed as he straightened his clothing.

Then with furrowed brows, he looked me straight in the eyes and threatened, "Well, understand this, son. If you can't stay away from her, I will make sure that she stays away from you… permanently."

He left me sitting against the wall as he turned and walked away as if nothing had even happened.

Chapter 24

Kendall

Three miserable weeks! It's been too long. I had given Cade his time to think, and the clock was ticking. Either he needed to decide that he was ready to re-commit, or I would be forced to go to Marcus and the elders. Something had to be done.

At least, he was no longer seeing Allison. He barely gives her the time of day at school, and not that I was checking, but there hadn't been anymore action on the pier since I caught them the last time. If Cade is seeing her, he's doing a really good job of covering his tracks. And if he thinks I'm going to keep pretending that we're still together for much longer, he's got another thing coming.

After an afternoon of shopping alone, I pulled into the driveway and noticed my mother's car in the garage. What was she doing home on Sunday afternoon? Usually she is off with the other female pack members, playing bridge or something. Who knows what those women do all day?

Mom was the last person I wanted to see. I have avoided her like the plague since Cade decided that we needed "a break," I spent most of my time with Shari, occasionally Becca, and I even went shopping with Cami once. If Mom knew that I haven't been with Cade for the last three weeks… well, I could only imagine what she'd have to say about it.

I wondered if Marcus was suspicious. Surely, he had noticed my sudden disappearance, which made me curious as to what Cade had told the alpha. Where had he been spending his time?

Grudgingly, I strolled up to our front porch, and just as I was about to open the door, Mom swung it open. "Oh, hey Kendall. You scared me to death! I'm heading over to Noel's. Would you like to come? I'm sure Cade will be there."

I shimmied around her to get inside and said, "No thanks. I have some homework to catch up on."

Mom turned around and followed me inside. "Homework? What? It can't wait?"

Without turning to face her, I lied, "No, Mom. It can't. I have an essay due tomorrow for English. I'll be in my room. Text me if you need anything."

I figured my measly excuse wouldn't be good enough for her, and, of course, I was right. "Okay, I know something is up. Are you and Cade fighting? You better not be causing problems, young lady!" I turned around to find her standing in the middle of the foyer with her hands on her hips.

Before I took my leave up the stairs, I tried to assure her, "Mom, everything is fine. Really. Ask Noel. I'm sure she will tell you that Cade and I are more in love than ever." That ought to keep her satisfied.

Almost satisfied, anyway. Before Mom headed out the door, she scolded, "Everything better be fine. You better not screw this up! I'm counting on you to keep that boy, or we will never be anything more than lowly pack members around here."

I didn't respond. As I stomped up the stairs, my mommy-dearest slammed the door behind her.

I made it up to my room just before my cell said, "Message received." I flipped it open to find a message from Cade.

We need to talk. Can I come over?

Surprise, frustration, and excitement all coursed through my body simultaneously. It was the first time he contacted me since everything fell apart. I texted him back, and he was at my door less than five minutes later.

After I invited him in, he followed me into the kitchen. "Hungry?" I asked, hoping to dispel the nervous energy in the air.

"No thanks. Can we sit down?"

We sat down at the kitchen table, and he scooted his chair closer to mine. His blood-shot eyes were glued to the floor. He looked like hell, but I figured it would be best to keep that thought to myself.

After an excruciating long moment of silence, Cade admitted, "I spent some time thinking, and I realized what a jerk I've been to you.

I'm sorry Kendall. Can we just forget the last three weeks and start over?"

These were the words I have been longing to hear, but what did he expect me to do? Just pick up where we left off like nothing had happened? Act like I hadn't seen him getting it on with another girl? Every fiber of my being wanted to tell him to screw off.

But I didn't. There was too much riding on me to make things right with the future alpha, no matter how much I wanted to physically hurt him for humiliating me like this. If anyone found out what has really been going on, I would be mortified.

Forcing my instincts to take a back seat, I smiled and said, "Okay. I've missed you." Then I kissed him. Really kissed him. Just to remind him what he's been missing. I said, "We have the house to ourselves. My mom won't be home for a few hours." Then, I straddled his lap and kissed him again.

Chapter 25

Allison

Even though I didn't hear from Cade all day yesterday, I have been on cloud nine since Saturday night. It was unbelievable. Secret dating certainly wasn't as good as for-real dating, but on Saturday night something changed between us.

Things were going to be different now, and before we left the lodge, Cade promised me that we would figure the whole Kendall thing out soon. He would find some way for us to be together. And I knew he would. Maybe that was what he was up to all day yesterday.

I knew in my heart that he cared about me just as much as I cared about him. Sneaking around for almost a month wasn't exactly how I imaged our relationship would begin, but if it was my only option, then I'll just have to wait it out.

Cade and Kendall couldn't pretend forever, could they? I wanted nothing more than to be able to hop in Sammy's car this morning, lean over, give Cade a kiss, and hold his hand on the way to school. It was so hard pretending like nothing was going on. At least, Kendall hadn't been riding to school with us. Apparently, Shari was her new personal chauffeur, which was just fine with me. How awkward would that be? Me, Cade, and Kendall all sitting next to each other like everything was normal.

I heard Sammy honking the horn in our driveway, so I rushed the finishing touches on my make-up and ran downstairs.

"Who are you trying to impress?" Aiden asked giving me a little eyebrow raise.

I gave him a dirty look, and said, "Shut up, Ad. Let's go."

I rushed out into the cold, thrilled to be next to Cade once again, and pulled the Suburban door open, only to have my heart completely crushed. I could hardly believe my eyes. Kendall was sitting next to

Cade, and to make matters worse, the she-devil had the nerve to smile at me. *Holy mother of God! WTF!*

They were holding hands! And, since Aiden grabbed the seat in the back, the only open seat was next to Kendall. Cade kept his eyes on the seat in front of him, refusing to look my way, which was probably a good thing. I quite possibly would have lost it had he made eye contact with me.

Trying my damnedest not to look like I might puke at any moment, I took my seat next to the bitch and slammed the door shut a little too hard.

"Sorry," I said under my breath.

The whole way to school, I kept secretly staring at Kendall and Cade's entwined fingers. Cade didn't say a single word to me; he didn't even acknowledge that I was in the car. Every time, Kendall would lean over and whisper in his ear, I felt bile rise up in my throat.

It's not that I really expected him to dump the bimbo "officially" already, but I honestly thought that he had more respect for me than to flaunt their relationship in front of me, especially now. Obviously, something was up, and Cade would better have an explanation.

By the time we pulled up in front of the school, I couldn't wait to get out of the car. I didn't look at anyone or talk to anyone; I hopped out of the car and hurried toward the entrance. I heard Aiden calling my name, but I kept walking straight ahead pretending I haven't heard him, and concentrated on getting to first period as soon as possible. I had to get away from them, away from all of them. Fast. Or I was going to have a complete breakdown in the middle of the commons. That, I couldn't afford.

I walked into room 302, and forced myself to muster up a smile when I saw Teagan.

"Hey, Alli-cat. Are you feeling okay? You look like you're about to be sick."

"I'm okay, I guess. I just don't feel all that great this morning," I admitted as I took my seat.

"Oh, maybe you should go to the nurse. Could be the flu," Teagan suggested.

I closed my eyes for a moment to concentrate on not throwing up my breakfast. What just happened? Cade and Kendall? Just like that? And he didn't even bother to tell me! How was I supposed to react? I laid my head down on my desk and tried not to let my emotions get the best of me.

I will not cry, I will not cry, I will not cry! I repeated silently over and over again.

"You sure you're okay?" Teagan asked again.

With my eyes still shut, I gave her a quick nod to let her know that I was alright. Teagan had really been the best these past few weeks. It was nice to have a real friend again, even if she was just a school friend. That was better than having no friends. I even told her about Cade. Well... I didn't tell her his name, but she knows that I had a secret thing going on. And the best thing about Teagan was that she didn't ask questions.

"Secret boyfriend troubles," she said. "I hope he isn't one of those testosterone-filled, alpha males that you have lunch with."

Before I could stop myself, a small chuckle escaped my lips. *Oh man, she doesn't know just how right she is,* I thought to myself.

"I really don't want to talk about it. Let's talk about something else. Anything else," I pleaded, finally opening my eyes.

"Sure, but talk to someone. Maybe one of those girls you eat lunch with. Or the counselor."

I gave her half a smile. "I wouldn't exactly call them my friends. We all live in the same neighborhood, and we ride together to school. That's it. And I'm not talking to the school counselor. Me and counselors don't mesh," I admitted.

Teagan started sorting through her school work and let the subject drop. Thank goodness, because I was fighting the urge to spill my guts to her about the whole sorted affair, and only because the teacher droned on and on until the dismissal bell rang, did I keep my secret safe. We didn't have the chance to say anything else to one another before the class was over. I surely would have regretted saying anything about Cade, but the need to tell someone was hard to resist. Teagan and I walked out together, and before she took off for her next class I asked, "Hey, do you mind if I sit with you at lunch today?" She smiled and said, "Sure thing, I'll save you a spot."

***

I made it to second period before Shari arrived. When she came in, she sat down at the desk next to mine and immediately said, "Hey Alli, we are going to grab a pizza after school if you want to come."

Completely shocked by the invite, I found myself scrambling for an excuse not to go. Before I even realized, a reply a bit too close to the truth slipped out. "Really? I don't know. I'm not sure that Kendall likes me very much."

Not that it should have surprised me, but she acted stunned that I didn't think of myself as Kendall's favorite person. "What? Well, no worries. Kendall's not coming. I think she has plans with Cade."

Just hearing his name pissed me off all over again, and I almost told Shari *thanks but no thanks*, but I didn't want to turn down my first invite to go out with the girls from the pack. I was having a hard enough time fitting in without giving them a reason to like me less, and I just would have gone home anyways, and obsessed over Kendall and Cade's revived relationship. I definitely needed something to take my mind off them and whatever it was they were doing after school.

"Okay, sure. How are we getting there?"

Shari smiled, and said, "Oh, I drove to school today. It's just going to be me, you, and Becca. Meet us after school out front."

Of course, I brooded over Cade the rest of the day and tried to unsuccessfully convince myself that it wasn't a big deal, to get over it, and that I should have seen it coming, but that wasn't working, so I just ended up feeling worse. I was an idiot to think that our relationship would work out. He dated me in secret, for God's sake. He was too ashamed to admit to anyone that he liked me, if he ever really did. I pretty much spent the majority of the day beating myself up for being so naïve.

Even though I sat with Teagan at lunch, I noticed that both Kendall and Cade were missing from the pack's table. Nothing could have diffused the anger burning inside me. I couldn't stop thinking about why they weren't at lunch. A private rendezvous at the library stacks? Or maybe outside under the bleachers?

Squeezing my eyes shut, I wished the images in my mind would take a hike, but that wasn't going to happen anytime soon, so I sat there in silence, letting it drive me crazy. I'm sure Teagan could tell, but she was nice enough not to say anything. Everyone else I encountered that day asked me what was wrong and if I was okay. Obviously, I was doing a sucky job of hiding my emotions.

After school, on my way out front, my nerves were getting the best of me. I couldn't believe I was going out for a pizza with Kendall's friends. How bizarre was that? I caught up with Aiden on my way out and let him know of my plans. He seemed... I don't know, pleased?

I saw Shari from across the way, and she waved me over.

"Hey Alli. You ready, girl?" Becca called, as if we had actually been friends since we first met. In reality, I think those five words were the most she ever bothered to say to me.

WTF! This was too weird. Why were they being all nice to me? My instincts were screaming that something fishy was going on, but I convinced myself that this was completely normal, and they were just trying to be friendly. This is what you do when you have friends, right?

We headed over to Gesseppi's pizza parlor, which was only a few miles from school.

The girls gabbed the whole way there. Though I wasn't exactly included in the conversation, I gave an occasional nod and giggle, so they knew I was listening. Once there, Shari ordered a large pepperoni pizza and drinks for all of us.

We got settled at a table, and as we waited for our pizza, Becca asked, "So Alli, how do you like being a werewolf?"

"I don't know. I mean, I guess it's better now that I know what's going on with me. For a while there, I thought I was either really sick or really crazy, you know?" I replied.

Shari smiled and said, "I bet. You probably thought you were running a fever, huh?"

"Yeah, I kept having hot flashes. That sucked, but the worst part of it all was all the smells in the air. Every time I turned around, something else was making me nauseous," I added.

As we all laughed, I couldn't believe how cool these girls were being, especially since neither of them had really talked to me much since the first night we arrived. I couldn't help but wonder what Kendall would think if she knew I was having pizza with her best friends.

"Aiden seems to be adjusting. I mean, he just kind of fits right in with a group of guys, who generally don't like newcomers. Plus, he is so hot," Shari said.

Just as I was about to tell them that Aiden didn't seem fazed by any of it, I heard the bells over the door ring, and turned to see who was walking in. *Oh shit! I thought she wasn't coming.*

Chapter 26

Kendall

"Hey chicas! And Alli. I guess I made it after all," I announced as I waltzed through the door.

The look on Allison's face was priceless. If only I had my iPhone ready to snap a photo. My day couldn't get much better. First, Cade decided to drop the little home-wrecker on her poor, pitiful ass, and now I get to rub it in her pretty, little face, and all in the same day. If I didn't know better, I would have thought it was my birthday.

After Alli wiped the shock off her face, she pushed her chair back from the table and said, "I'll be right back." She hurried toward the bathroom. Probably to go throw-up. Poor thing, doesn't seem to handle stress well. She walked around all day looking like her favorite cat got ran over.

"Okay honey! Hurry back, we have so much to talk about," I responded as sweetly as I could stomach.

As soon as the bathroom door closed, I turned to my girls and said, "Hurry, grab her stuff. Let's get out of here."

"We can't just leave her here with nothing, Kendall. How will she get home?" Shari asked.

"I don't care. The little ho-bag is lucky I didn't rip out her throat. Now grab her purse and backpack, Shari!"

Without another word, they grabbed Allison's stuff, and we ran out of the pizza joint before anyone noticed or had a chance to say anything. Leaving her stranded was nothing, compared to what I wanted to do to her, but she would definitely get the hint. She might think that she "loves" Cade—ugh!—but he is mine. He was promised to me a long time ago, and I will not back down. This will teach her not to touch anything that belongs to me. If she wants to be a member of this pack, she needs to know her place. At the bottom!

Chapter 27

Allison

I was only in the restroom for like three minutes, but when I came out, everyone was gone. I ran to the window just in time to see Kendall and the rest of the girls peeling out of the parking lot. I could only imagine what they were saying to one another as they took off for the estate, leaving me stranded twenty minutes from home without my purse and my backpack.

Completely mortified, I explained to our waiter that I had been left behind without any money. He took pity on me and was kind enough to accept my promise to come back tomorrow and pay for the pizza and drinks, plus a hefty tip. He knew as well as I did that I was the victim of a cruel, cruel prank, and he was kind enough not to make me go in to detail about why they left me standing there. The waiter offered to let me use the phone, but I didn't have any of the new numbers memorized, and to be honest, I was too embarrassed to admit to anyone what had happened.

I stood there at the edge of the parking lot, staring down at the long road home, contemplating my next move. I had no phone, no money, and no transportation. I did the only thing I could do; I started walking. I followed the road for what seemed like hours. I must have walked five miles, and with each step, I became more and more enraged. By the time I made it to the city limits sign, I was not only fuming, but freezing, tired, hungry, frustrated, and hurt. To make things even worse, I was wearing brand new shoes that were absolutely killing my feet. With my knuckles clenched and my jaw tight, I was ready to draw blood. Cade and these bitches have messed with the wrong damn girl. Were they not listening when Aiden told them about me and my reputation at my old school? Were they stupid? Obviously they were.

I picked up my pace and tried to breathe slowly in and out. My chest was so tight that it hurt to breathe. Suddenly, I stopped in mid-step.

"Oh shit! Not now," I said under my breath, recognizing the familiar pains shooting through my stomach. I doubled-over, gripping my gut. I needed to get off the main road fast. Even though it had already become dark, I could not risk changing into a wolf right here in the middle of the highway.

I walked as fast as I could, focusing on calming down, and slowing my breathing, trying to prolong the inevitable. This was so not good. I made it to the tree line that signaled the end of the city just in time. I doubled over in pain once again; then before I knew it, I was down on all fours.

In this form, with this body and all the speed I could gather, I ran. I dashed the entire way back to the estate. I didn't slow down once. I didn't take time to notice all the new scents. I couldn't think of anything except ripping Kendall Stuart to shreds.

As I approached our house, I saw her. Kendall. My vision tunneled until all I could see was her. I finally slowed down, but not before I was only a few feet away. Acting on instinct, I hunched down, bared my teeth at her, and growled. I knew that she was frightened. I could smell it on her, and it only made me want to attack her even more.

It was only when I heard Kendall's name shouted from nearby did I pause and take in my surroundings. I had been so focused on kicking Kendall's ass that somehow I missed the crowd of people gathered on my front porch.

Holy shit! This wasn't good!

Before I could figure out what to do next, Marcus and three others shifted in mid-air as they launched themselves toward me. The shock and fear of seeing four massive werewolves coming after me must have triggered my immediate change back because just as they reached me, I was human again. Human and completely, butt-ass naked.

***

Oh-my-God! This cannot be happening! Seriously!

I stood there literally dazed and confused, trying to cover myself with my hands, when Cade came rushing my way to throw his jacket over my bare shoulders. I quickly shrugged the jacket on over my naked body as I jerked away from him. Looking him straight in the eyes, I said, "Don't touch me!"

Trying desperately to avoid all other eye contact, I hurried toward the front door as fast as my naked, human legs could carry me. Unable to believe that everyone, my mom, dad, brother, Cade, Kendall, and just about every other wolf in the pack was staring at me in horror, I sure as hell wasn't about to hang around and explain myself. Thank God my grandparents weren't there. Gram would have had a conniption fit.

I ignored the people calling my name. Really, what did they expect me to do? Stand around in only a jacket and chit-chat? I had just made it up to my room when I heard the front door open and close downstairs. I quickly threw on a t-shirt and jeans just as I heard a small knock on my door.

"Alli? Baby, can I come in?" my dad called from outside my door.

I considered not answering, but figured it wasn't his fault that I shifted from wolf to human in front of everyone and ended up flashing my new pack.

"Yeah, you can come in."

Dad slowly opened the door and peeked inside as if he was worried that I might actually still be naked.

"You okay, honey?"

I couldn't hide my irritation. What a stupid question. "What do you think, Dad? The whole pack just saw me in my birthday suit."

"We barely saw anything. Really. I think everyone was more shocked that you were a wolf than anything else."

"Yeah right, Dad. I'm not a complete idiot."

"Well, anyways… you want to tell me what happened?"

"I don't really want to talk about it. It is just so humiliating."

"Come on, Al. You're going to have to tell us at some point."

I so didn't want to have this conversation right now. The entire incident was totally humiliating. Kendall must be in freakin' heaven.

First she embarrasses me; then I embarrass myself. How am I ever going to face those people again? And Omigod, Cade of all people.

Finally, I agreed to tell Dad the whole story. The invitation, my reservations, the pizza place, the angry walk home, my transformation, and well, he witnessed the rest. I could literally see his anger building as my story continued. First his face reddened, then he clinched his knuckles, but I knew he was really upset when he stood and began to pace. Yes, Dad was pissed! Really, really pissed. I couldn't remember ever seeing my dad with that much rage in his eyes. Without looking at me, he turned toward my door and said through gritted teeth, "I'll be right back, honey," and he left my room.

I just sat there, my mind reeling. I couldn't believe this was happening to me. I really could have killed Kendall. Surely, there can't be a bigger bitch on the entire planet. How could anyone be so evil?

I lay back on my bed trying to convince myself to stay put. All I wanted to do was go sit by the window and peek out so I could see what was going on, but, for obvious reasons, I decided it was best to wait for someone to come tell me what happened after I fled the scene.

After thirty painfully long minutes, my mom showed up at my door with an oh-honey-I-feel-so-bad-for-you look on her face. My first instinct was to slam the door, but I didn't. Keeping my temper in check, I asked her to sit down and tell me how much drama my little escapade caused.

She sort of half-way laughed before she said, "Of course, I'll tell you what happened, but first I want to know about your transformation. Was that your first time?"

I'm not sure why I told her the truth, but I did.

"Actually, no. It happened one other time a few weeks ago."

I left out the other night when Cade helped me change and we went running together.

"What! Why didn't you tell me?" she asked, not bothering to hide her disappointment in me.

"I don't know Mom. I was so freaked out by the whole thing. I just decided to keep it to myself. Plus, it felt, I don't know, kind of personal. I didn't think about the fact that I might get so ticked off that I'd turn into a wolf and try to attack Kendall. It's not like I could have known that could happen. Let's face it Mom, I don't know much more about being a werewolf than I do about rocket science."

She may have looked at me incredulously, but she knew I was right. She hadn't told me anything about the change: what to expect, how to control it, yada, yada, yada. But, I get it. I should have told someone. As I tried to assure her that I will be more open about my were-life, Mom droned on and on about needing to be honest, and how Aiden and I needed to learn how to control the transformation as soon as possible, blah, blah, blah. Doesn't she realize that the only thing I really cared about at that moment was what the hell had happened outside?

After she finally paused to take a breath, I cut in, "So, are you going to tell me what happened out there, or not?"

"Well, okay long story short, all hell broke loose. Shari confessed about her part in the plan to ditch you. Marcus told the girls, including Kendall, that he was extremely disappointed in them, and their punishments would be announced at the pack meeting tomorrow night. Well, and then your dad came out yelling up a storm about how those girls are treating his baby girl."

Oh freakin' great. How embarrassing! I knew my dad meant well, but damn! Could he have made this anymore humiliating? And now we have to relive the entire ordeal again at a meeting. Just in case the whole pack didn't see it first hand, they'll be sure to get a play-by-play at the meeting.

"Can't I skip this meeting, Mom? It's just too embarrassing." I asked, praying she would take pity on me.

"Afraid not, baby. Marcus wants everyone there, and he sounded serious."

She put her hand on my shoulder and said, "It will pass, I promise. Do you want some dinner?"

I looked at her like she was nuts for even asking. As if I could eat after practically streaking through the estate. Just the thought of food made me want to vomit.

With a deep sigh, she tilted her head to the side like she always did when she couldn't make me feel better. "Well, if you're not going to eat, why don't you try to relax? Maybe a nap," she said, and then kissed the top of my head.

***

The next morning, I refused to ride with the evil were-herd. Plus the thought of seeing Cade after… well, after him seeing me in all my naked glory, was horrifying. I begged Mom to drive me, but Dad stepped up and offered to take me.

Knowing how slow Dad drove, I pleaded to Mom with my eyes until she finally gave in and said, "I will take you and Aiden to school this morning. You shouldn't have to ride with that awful girl, in fact, we might think about getting a second car."

I couldn't contain my smile. A second car would be absolutely perfect. Aiden and I wouldn't have to car pool to school anymore, and I wouldn't need to be around the bitch from hell. But… I wouldn't get to see Cade either, not that I should want to. Maybe *not* seeing Cade was just what I needed.

All morning and on the way to school, Aiden wouldn't even look at me. He avoided me at all costs last night and this morning. Then he didn't say a word to me on the drive to school. I should have just asked him what was wrong, but I didn't want to make things even more awkward. All I could figure was that he must have been embarrassed. It's not every day that you see your sister butt-ass naked.

On our way into the building, I couldn't take the silent treatment any longer and finally said, "So, are you like never speaking to me again or what?"

He didn't look my way, but at least he responded. "Sorry, Al. I'm just a little freaked out by the whole thing. But just so you know, I'm on your side. I hope Kendall gets in some serious trouble. She deserves it. I can't believe she'd do something so shitty."

"Are you sure that is all that's wrong with you? You sure you're not just embarrassed that you saw me naked?"

"Yeah, I guess. Well, no not really."

"What else is wrong then?" I asked, pretty sure that I couldn't have managed to piss him off about anything else. I practically locked myself in my room last night.

Aiden shifted from foot to foot and looked around to make sure no one could hear him. "Okay, but don't laugh, and you better not tell anyone." He paused for a moment to make sure I agreed with his terms, so I nodded my head. Finally Aiden admitted, "I can't help but wonder why you became a wolf already and I haven't. I'm older. It should have happened to me first. Right? It's like I'm slow or something. Like I'm a were-tard."

I had to laugh at that. Poor Aiden thinks he's a learning-disabled wolf.

"Don't worry, Ad. Your time will come. I just hope for your sake that it doesn't happen in front of the whole pack."

That made him smile a little. We parted ways, and I headed to my locker trying at all costs to avoid everyone. When I opened my locker, a note fell to the ground at my feet. I picked it up and read:

> *Allison,*
> *Meet me at the gazebo on the pier after the meeting tonight. We need to talk.*
> *—Cade*

Upon reading the note I was flooded with mixed emotions. On one hand, I couldn't wait to see Cade again, but on the other, I was still so hurt and humiliated over how he treated me. So I did the only thing I could think of; I crumpled up the note and threw it into my locker. Taking a deep breath, I slammed my locker shut and went to class.

Chapter 28

Cade

I stood outside Kendall's front door thinking about how incredibly screwed up this all was. How was I supposed to act like everything was okay between us? Being with her in front of Alli, and seeing how hurt Alli was, almost killed me. I can only pray that Alli got my note today, and decides to meet me tonight. I have to tell her just how sorry I am, and at least try to explain myself.

I was about to knock when Kendall came out, "Hey, baby. Were you just going to stand there all night?" she said playfully.

She actually had the nerve to bounce out of her house like everything was good. She even tried to kiss me, but I moved away from her.

"What the hell were you thinking, Kendall? How could you do that to Alli? How could you do that to anyone? I did exactly what you wanted me to do. I stopped seeing her. I promised to never see her again, then you go and leave her stranded twenty minutes from home? What is wrong with you?" I yelled before I turned and walked away from her.

"It was just a prank, baby. It's really no big deal. It's not my fault she can't take a joke. How was I supposed to know she would turn into some psycho-wolf and try to attack me? And speaking of that, why aren't you mad at her for trying to hurt me?" she shouted.

That stopped me. "You're kidding right? You want me to be mad at Allison?" I asked as I turned around to look at her. She can't be serious!

Kendall put her hands on her hips and said, "Oh, poor ALLISON! I'm so freakin' sick of hearing about her. Now you need to put on a happy face and walk me to the meeting, Cade. Don't make this harder than it has to be."

I just rolled my eyes and decided to keep my mouth shut. It didn't matter what I said. Kendall lives in Kendall-land and that was that. I turned and headed toward the lodge without another word. Unbelievably enough, Kendall followed behind me and before I knew it, she was walking next to me like we were heading to the meeting together. It was at that moment that I realized a few things. I was beginning to hate the girl next to me—the one I was supposed to love. I was losing the girl I wanted to be with—the one I was pretty sure I was falling in love with—and as long as I was the future alpha, my life was not my own.

Was being the alpha of this pack worth giving up the freedom to make my own decisions? How long will I be able to stand by and let my future be decided for me?

Chapter 29

Allison

Sitting with my mom on my right and Aiden on my left, I was glad to be sandwiched between people who genuinely loved me. I was not easily intimidated, but being surrounded by unfamiliar werewolves, all eyeing the newbies, was almost more than I could handle. And the fact that half of them had seen me naked, didn't make things any easier.

It was all a bit bizarre. I kind of assumed the meeting would take place out in the woods, with the pack gathered around a big bonfire, but that wasn't the case. We gathered in the main lodge, a huge meeting hall that kind of resembled a court house in DC. I guess they took this kind of thing pretty seriously.

I spotted my arch-nemesis and Cade walking in... together. The sight of them with each other made my heart hurt. I had to take a deep breath, so I wouldn't completely lose it in front of everyone. I couldn't believe that after Kendall all but left me for dead at the pizza place, Cade would still waltz right in here with her, as if nothing had even happened. I figured he would, at the very least, be pissed at her. Inconspicuously, I peeked toward their direction and saw that they were holding hands. So he was obviously still with Kendall, while I have a note from him in my pocket asking me to meet him later. Suddenly, I wasn't too thrilled to find out what he wanted to talk about.

Damn him if he thinks for one second that I'm going to continue to sneak around with him. I may have went back to get the letter out of my locker. But so what? That didn't mean that I was going to fall right back into his no-good-lying-cheating arms.

Before I fully worked myself into a tizzy, my little internal tirade was cut short by Marcus as he walked to the front of the pack to begin his meeting. I expected him to bang a gavel or something, but instead he simply cleared his throat and suddenly everyone was silent.

Marcus took command of the room with his booming voice an instant later.

"Fellow pack members, we gather here today to discuss some very important news from the community. But first, I want to take this opportunity to officially welcome the new members to our pack. They have been with us for almost a month now, and I know most of you have met them already, but let's take a moment to formally introduce them."

As the alpha turned his attention to us, the entire crowd turned in unison and all eyes were staring in our direction.

"Many of you remember Lily. Let's welcome her home."

The pack all clapped politely as Mom's cheeks reddened.

"And she has brought her family with her: her husband, Paul, and her children, Allison and Aiden."

I looked over and saw my grandparents beaming with pride, so I gave a little half-wave and a smile to the crowd, trying to ignore the fact that most of these people had been more than "formally" introduced to me already. It was safe to assume that they won't forget my name anytime soon, though I will most likely be forever known as *that naked chick*.

The group quieted as if on cue, and Marcus continued. "Lily will be our webmaster for our company, and Paul has made quite a name for himself in the music industry, so he, of course, will continue his work in that field. We are happy to have you all here, and hope that you will make this your permanent home."

After another short applause from the pack, Marcus got down to business.

"We've been informed by our neighboring pack that one of their more unsavory members has gone rogue and may be seeking membership with a new pack. Now, this character was awaiting an appearance in front of the Elders to plead his case. He was to be tried for domestic assault against one of his fellow pack members, but before that could occur, he disappeared. His name is Damon Jennings, but I would imagine he changed his name to avoid being found. He is considered to be extremely dangerous. I ask that if you see anyone suspicious in or around the estate that you come directly to me. And it's definitely not a good idea to be out at night alone."

Mom leaned over and whispered, "I didn't want to scare you honey, but that's why they almost attacked you. When you were missing, everyone assumed the worst, so they were quick to jump on an unfamiliar wolf."

Before the meeting ended, Marcus made Kendall, Shari, and Becca stand and face the pack. He publicly issued their punishment for mistreatment of a fellow pack member—me, and he put them on a mandatory curfew. Each of them had to be home by ten o'clock every night for the remainder of the month. Kendall, being the cold-hearted bitch that she is, showed absolutely no emotion on her face, while Shari and Becca both looked mortified.

***

Relief, and since I'm being honest, a little excitement washed over me when the meeting was finally over. I really couldn't wait to go meet Cade. I needed to know for sure where we stood.

At least, now that Kendall had to go straight home, I wouldn't have to worry about her joining us. I had no idea why he wanted to meet, and even though I knew a lot needed to be said, I wasn't sure what. My first question, of course, was going to be what was up with him and Kendall's rekindled relationship. The one thing I was sure of was that I wasn't up for participating in any love triangle, or being the other girl any longer. I was done sneaking around.

Once we got home and everyone was settled, I snuck out of the mud room and headed toward the pier. I figured it would be easier that way, being that we had all just been warned about being out alone, and I couldn't really explain that I was going to meet Cade.

The cold bit through my jeans and overcoat. While Mom continued to assure me that my werewolf body temperature would help me get used to the cold, I wasn't convinced that I'd ever get used to the weather here. New Mexico was quickly turning into a frigid hell on earth. But just as I spotted Cade waiting for me near the water, a rush of heat shot through me, instantly warming me.

He turned around and smiled. God, he was beautiful.

My pace quickened. I couldn't help but rush toward him. He was a compulsion, a need… a need that I wanted more than anything not to need.

Cade met me at the end of the pier, and as we reached each other, we just stood there as if there were no words for what we were feeling. For seconds, maybe minutes, we stared into each other's eyes, and then before anything was said, Cade wrapped his arm tightly around my body. My arms, clearly with a mind of their own, followed suit, and we embraced, soaking in each other's scent.

He started to look up, to say whatever it was that he needed to say, but I didn't give him the chance. I reached up, my hands wrapping around his neck, and I pulled his lips to mine. I was not gentle. I was done waiting for him. I needed this. A millisecond later, Cade deepened the kiss. He took control, pulling me closer and pressing his body against mine. Nothing had ever felt so right. Then suddenly, he jerked away, leaving me breathless and instantly cold.

"We can't do this Allison. I'm sorry. I can't deny that I have feelings for you, but we just can't be together. Not now, probably never," he said, but I was so stunned that I could hardly make out his words.

"I know it is hard to understand, but my future has already been planned out for me. I will be the alpha soon, and Kendall has been chosen to be my mate."

He paused, waiting for me to say something, but I couldn't get the words in the right order in my head, so I just stared at him in disbelief.

"I tried to explain before how things work on the estate, Allison. At eighteen, we are considered adults. And it won't be long before I'm expected to take over the pack. You may think it's absurd, but I have to start acting like an adult, and that means I have to do what's right for the pack."

He took a breath, and I took it as an opportunity to interrupt. Thankfully, my ability to speak had returned. "Are you finished with your monologue? Christ, Cade, how long have you been rehearsing that? You are truly unbelievable. Do you honestly think that Kendall is what's best for the pack? You can't be serious?" I yelled.

"Look, it's already planned. I can't do anything to change it. I'm sorry."

"No, please don't apologize. I can't believe this. You know what? You two deserve each other. She's a bitch, and you're a coward! I hope you will be really happy together."

Before he could respond, I turned and ran away from him. I ran until I could hardly breathe or see through my tears.

Chapter 30

Cade

Allison was right. I was being a coward.

While I kept some space between us, I followed her to make sure she got home okay. Did I try to talk to her? Did I try to make her understand my situation? Did I grab her and show her just what she means to me? No. I just followed her. Watching her, and knowing that she hates me, that she's crying because of me, made me sick to my stomach.

If my dad knew I was following Allison, he would kill me. If only I knew what he was really capable of, what lengths he would go to keep me from going down the path that he has forbidden. If any other member of the pack went against the alpha's demands, he would be banished. Would he do that to Allison? Would he do that to his own son? He must have noticed the obvious connection that Allison and I have. Kendall sure noticed. Why would he want me to marry Kendall when he knows I don't even love her?

Allison was going in the wrong direction. I tried to stay far enough behind her so that she wouldn't hear or see me. Since I was bordering on being a stalker, I couldn't just tell her to turn around, but I didn't plan on watching her freeze to death trying to find her own way either. Just as I was about to change forms to get closer to her, I heard voices not far away approaching Allison. I kept her in sight, but made sure I was far enough so that the others couldn't see me.

Chapter 31

Allison

I don't know for how long I ran, but I didn't stop until I was sure I was far away from Cade. I wanted to get off this estate, out of New Mexico, and back to my old, pitiful life back in Texas. Anything would be better than this.

How could he? I snuck around with him for weeks thinking things would change. I'm just like one of those stupid mistresses; one who truly believes that the lying sack of shit she is fooling around with is actually going to leave his wife. Could I have been more of an idiot?

It's complicated! That is such bullshit!

Finally I slowed down, needing to catch my breath and get my bearings. Tears continued to stream down my face as I gulped in the winter air. The fact that I was crying over that bastard made me so angry that I just ended up crying harder. With my hands on my knees, I tried to control my sobs and catch my breath.

I looked around to see if I could recognize anything that might point me in the direction of my house, but everything looked exactly the same. Huge trees blocked my view of the lake and the houses surrounding it. I couldn't believe that I didn't recognize anything. Being a werewolf has certainly not improved my sense of direction. I was about to throw myself to the forest floor and have a full-out tantrum when I heard voices. Quickly, I wiped my tears away and tried to get myself under control before anyone saw me. I really didn't want to be caught crying my eyes out. The voices were getting closer, and I decided that one of the voices belonged to Luke, the guy I met at the bonfire.

Finally, the group came into view. "Hey Alli. What are you doing way out here?" Luke said.

"Oh hey, Luke. I guess I got a little turned around," I said trying to play it cool. "Okay, who am I kidding? I'm completely lost," I added.

Luke was with two other guys. The tallest, Gage, I had met before, but the other guy was completely unfamiliar. It was no secret that I was upset, but at least they were all nice enough not to ask about it.

"Hey, it happens. This place is pretty big, and it's easy to get a little lost," Gage said.

Standing in the middle of the woods with two guys who were practically strangers, both of whom had seen me naked I might add, and one complete stranger, was a tad unnerving. I was wracking my brain to think of something to say, but nothing was coming.

"Oh hey, this is Dylan. He's new to town, like you," Gage said.

Dylan stuck out his hand and said, "Nice to meet you…"

"Allison, or Alli," I said filling in the blank.

Dylan smiled, held my hand for just a bit too long, and I could have sworn he took a whiff of me. Guess that means he's a were, but it was still a little freaky to have some random guy sniffing you in the woods.

The guys reeked of booze and pot, and even though Luke had been nothing but nice to me, I couldn't help but feel a little uncomfortable.

We stood around and made small talk for a few minutes, and then out of nowhere, Dylan announced, "Guys, it's been real, but I'm out of here."

Without waiting around for goodbyes, he took off through the trees.

Immediately after Dylan's peculiar departure, Gage unexpectedly grabbed me by the shoulders, spun me around, and said, "Head that way, and you'll run right into the lake."

But before he let go of my shoulders, I think he sniffed me too. What's up with these guys?

I took my leave and headed toward the trees hoping that Gage was right.

Chapter 32

Kendall

"So, what do you have to say for yourself, young lady," my mom asked as she made herself a drink. A stiff one. She only broke out the vodka when she had an especially rough day. I watched as she added a splash of orange juice to her glass.

She made me sit down at the kitchen table just like she did when I was little. After Marcus's little speech, I was in no mood for her lecture. "Nothing. I have nothing to say, Mom."

"Nothing? You can't be serious. What? You think your behavior should just go unpunished? I should take that new car away. That's what I should do. Girls like you shouldn't be driving around in a brand new car. That's what the other women here would say." Mom took a gulp of her drink, and the look on her face told me it was strong, even for her.

I shifted in my chair. What did she expect me to say? What was there to say? I screwed up. I should have known Allison would snitch. What I didn't expect was that she'd go all schizo-wolf on me, and then shift right there in front of everyone. One very naked Allison, right there for the whole pack to see. It was actually kind of funny. Seeing her there completely humiliated was definitely worth being on lockdown.

It wouldn't last anyway. Mom is drunk as a skunk by ten o'clock most nights, and hardly notices whether I'm here or not. Does Marcus really plan on checking to make sure I'm tucked away in bed each night? Becca and Shari might adhere to his bullshit rules, but I plan on doing whatever I want.

"Mom, just give it a rest. I'm being punished by the pack, okay? You don't have to take away my car. I won't screw up again!"

She took another drink and headed toward me. "You better watch your tone. The fact is, what you did was stupid. If you have a problem with the Wright girl, that's fine, but whatever you do, you need to be sure it doesn't come back on you."

So, there it was. Her real problem was that I made her look bad today. She doesn't care what I do, as long as it doesn't affect her.

"Fine, Mom. Don't worry. I won't make the same mistake again."

"You better not, Kendall. How am I supposed to show my face around the estate tomorrow? After what you did? I'll have to personally apologize to Lillian now."

"Can I go to bed now?"

She sat down at the table to finish her drink. "Yes, but you better make sure that everything is okay with you and Cade tomorrow. Your relationship has been rocky enough without you screwing things up even further. I saw how he ran over to cover Allison up. Are you sure you are telling me everything?"

I stood up and headed out of the kitchen. "Cade and I are fine, Mother."

But before I made it out of earshot, she said, "Why don't you invite him over tomorrow night? I'll be out, so you two can be alone. Maybe some alone time is just what you two need. If you know what I mean."

Chapter 33

Allison

Ahh! The lake. Finally!

I never thought I would be so happy to see this God-forsaken body of water. I was on the verge of freezing to death, and still very well might if I don't make it home soon. At least my brisk walk through the woods had enabled me to calm down… some. I followed the edge of the water with no clue as to how far I still needed to go to reach the warmth of my house.

I trudged along for what felt like forever with my internal dialogue on repeat. *I hate Cade, I'm going to kill Kendall, being a werewolf totally sucks, I hate Cade, I'm going to kill Kendall, being a werewolf totally sucks…*

Then I saw it. A beacon of hope. The pier, that I would now rather forget existed, came into view, and while I was slightly repulsed by the sight of it remembering all that had come to pass there, I knew my home was not far off.

I tromped a few steps farther when I heard the faint sounds of footsteps coming from behind me. *Go away Cade.* I turned around to tell him to go f–himself, but stopped dead in my tracks. It wasn't Cade. It was Dylan, the one who was with Luke and Gage earlier, and this guy's creepy-factor was off the charts.

"Hey, Alli. I didn't scare you did I?" he asked sounding concerned, but the sinister smile spreading across his face gave me the feeling that he just might have wanted me to say yes.

"Surprised is more like it. Are you following me?"

"You would like that, wouldn't you?" he said moving closer toward me.

Ewww! He can't be serious.

"Whatever," I quipped as I turned around and started walking away.

"Where are you rushing off to? To find Cade?"

That got my attention. What the hell did he know about Cade and me? More than anything, I wanted to find out what he meant, but my gut was telling me to get the hell away from him and quickly. So, I held my questions at bay and gave him my best kiss-my-ass glare before I continued on my way.

"Oh, I'm not supposed to know. Am I? Maybe you shouldn't wander around reeking of the guy if you want to keep it a secret... just sayin'," Dylan so eloquently suggested.

I kept charging ahead, hoping he might take a hint and go away.

Without warning, Dylan grabbed me by the arm and whirled me around to face him.

"What the fu—"

"Ah-ah-ah watch that tongue of yours," Dylan chided.

"Get your hands off of me! What the hell is your problem?" I said faking a little bravado.

To be honest, I was scared of this guy. He seemed to know way too much about me, and I knew absolutely nothing about him, except that I didn't like him at all. My human instincts wanted me to run, but the wolf in me knew that running could make things worse. So I stood there facing this stranger in the middle of the night, waiting for him to say something else.

He put his hands up in the air, as if he were under arrest and said, "No problem. I don't like leftovers anyway."

Excuse me? Now I was pissed! Did he actually just call me leftovers? He might be a guy and a werewolf, but at that point, I was ready to kick his furry ass.

"You're kidding, right? Look, I don't know what you think you know, but you need to turn around and walk away," I said taking a step toward him, trying to play the tough-were-girl part.

"You're a lively little thing, aren't you? I can see why Cade's smitten with you. It's really a tragic story, you and Cade. Very Romeo and Juliet-ish," he said.

Knowing it was best to ignore his absurd comment, I began to walk home again, but I only made it a few feet before the psycho-were caught up with me, grabbed me by my upper-arms, and pulled me up against him. With his chest pressed firmly against my back, he inhaled deeply and whispered, "I wasn't quite done with you, pup. If you run from me, I will catch you. And I won't be gentle."

His hot breath on my neck was causing the sick, twitchy feeling deep in my stomach to begin. I tried to focus on my breathing because I knew that if I changed right here in front of Dylan, he would too. I didn't even want to think of all the bad things that could come of that.

"Come on baby, change for me. You know you want to. Let's play," he dared.

A rustle in the trees behind us averted Dylan's attention. He pushed me away and turned around, only to find Cade rushing toward him with fury in his eyes.

"You wanna play, bitch? Come play with me," Cade roared just before he pounded Dylan in the face, so hard that he fell to the ground. Immediately, Cade was on top of Dylan holding him down by his neck.

"Touch her again and I will rip your fucking throat out. Do you understand me, dog?"

Cade got up and told Dylan to get the hell off his estate. Without another word, Dylan staggered to his feet, changed forms, and ran off into the woods.

Cade and I just stood there face to face. I could tell the anger and leftover adrenaline was slowly fading from his body as he stared down at me. He didn't say anything and neither did I. There was nothing left to say. Finally, I turned and walked home. I didn't look back, but I knew that Cade would follow me until I was safely inside.

Chapter 34

Allison

"Hey, Al, get dressed. Let's go shopping," Aiden said through my bedroom door. Ever since the horrible "seeing my sister naked" incident occurred, he never, ever, enters my room without being 100 percent sure that I am completely covered.

"No! I don't feel good," I moaned as I turned over and threw my covers over my head. After getting lost in the woods and being ambushed by Dylan, the were-freak, I wasn't feeling so hot, and the last thing I wanted to do was get out of bed.

"Can I come in?" he asked.

"Yes, but you can't stay long. I'm dying here and would appreciate some privacy."

Aiden walked in and sat at the end of my bed. "Alli, please go shopping with me. I have worn everything I own at least three times. It's getting embarrassing," he whined.

"God you're such a girl," I said from underneath my covers.

"Come on seriously. It's snowing; don't make me drive by myself. I hate driving in the snow. You know it freaks me out."

I threw my blanket off and conceded, "You can be such a puss! Give me ten minutes, and you totally owe me for this."

Eleven minutes later, I was walking down the stairs regretting my decision to join Aiden on a shopping expedition. "Let's go if we're going," I yelled at Aiden, who was fumbling around in the kitchen.

"Okay, but Mom wants us to drop this off at Gram's on the way," Aiden said holding up the envelope.

"What is it?"

"No idea. Come on, let's go," Aiden said bundling up like it was forty degrees below zero outside.

Gram was sitting on her porch and Grandfather was pushing snow off the driveway with some kind of broom-shovel thing when we pulled up.

"God! I hope Dad never makes me do that. It's freezing out here," Aiden said to Grandfather.

"Puss," Grandfather said under his breath. But I heard him.

"Hey, that's what I called him," I told him. Grandfather and I shared a quick smile before he went back to shoveling.

Gram walked down, and I gave her the envelope from Mom. She took it, but grabbed my hand and held it up to her nose. This was all too weird. She actually took a whiff of my wrist.

"Why do you smell weird? You kind of smell… ill. Are you feeling alright?" she asked.

"I'm fine, Gram. Really," I said.

"Where are you two off to today," Grandfather asked, without looking up from his work.

"I'm driving him to the mall. He doesn't like to drive in the snow," I said, which caused Aiden to shoot me with an I'm-so-going-to-kill-you-later stare. I knew he'd be pissed, but he did owe me, and I always collect.

Grandfather chuckled and Gram shook her head. Aiden just stood there and shrugged his shoulders. "Good gracious, Aiden, we need to toughen you up," Gram said with a laugh.

"Well, see ya soon, okay," I said. I didn't know if I was supposed to hug them, or shake their hands, or just get in the car. I opted for getting in the car.

***

Why was I out of bed? When humans feel like the walking dead, they don't go shopping. They stay in bed! But no, I was driving the bawl-bag to the mall, even though I felt like I have been run over by a Mack truck. Of course, I didn't have a clue what was wrong with me. All I knew was that I woke up with a killer headache, and felt like I hadn't eaten in days. And oddly enough, the last thing I wanted was food. Just the thought of it, made my stomach churn.

But nothing was going to stop Aiden from getting his new wardrobe, and ever since Mom bought the new car, he has been too chicken to drive in the snow. So here I was driving my *big* brother to the mall.

It took every ounce of energy for me to get out of the car and walk through the parking lot. I knew this would be no short venture being that Aiden was far worse than any girl I've ever met when it came to shopping.

It was no big surprise that he had to go into every single store even though his poor little sister felt like she was going to drop at any moment. After following Aiden around for a while, I found that sitting on the benches outside of the stores helped a bit. When Aiden waltzed out of Hollister with half the store tucked neatly inside a few trendy bags, I let him know that I would meet him in a half-hour at Macy's. I was badly in need of some version of hot, sweet caffeine before I passed out.

On my way to Starbucks, I saw Teagan, in a Sephora apron, taking a break at the scattered tables outside the coffee shop. I wandered up and as cheerfully as I could stand, said, "Hey girl! I didn't know you worked at the mall."

She jumped like I had startled her, then smiled and replied, "Lucky me, huh. It kind of sucks, but I do get a 25 percent discount. What are you up to? You want to sit? You look… tired."

Lovely, I must have looked as bad as I felt.

"Yeah, I don't feel so great, but my brother dragged me out here. Can you believe that my big, bad brother is afraid to drive in the snow?"

I sat down and we chatted for a few minutes before Teagan brought up the last thing in the world that I wanted to talk about.

"So what's up with your mystery man?"

"I don't know. I guess it's over between us," I said.

"Ahhh, that sucks. What happened?" Teagan asked.

"It turns out that he is not as available as I had previously thought. He has a girlfriend, a mean one, and he has no plans of leaving her." I felt myself beginning to sulk and suggested, "Can we just talk about something else?" Suddenly, I felt even worse as my stomach cramped like someone was twisting my insides into a giant pretzel knot.

Teagan shrugged her shoulders and replied, "Okay, but if you change your mind…"

I felt bad for not confiding in Teagan. She was the closest friend I had, but what in the world would I say? I couldn't tell her about the psycho-werewolf who accosted me in the woods the other night, or about falling for my were-pack's soon-to-be-alpha who is "promised" to the horrible girl she told me about on the first day of school, or about how that horrible girl humiliated me in front of the entire pack, or about how I feel like I have the flu or something, yet I'm not even supposed to be able to get sick. Yeah, there wasn't much I *could* confide in my new human friend.

So, instead, I opted to change the subject entirely. "Hey, Thanksgiving break is coming up, so if you are staying in town, maybe we can hang out? Catch a movie or something. Maybe do some Christmas shopping."

"Umm…I don't know. I have a lot of studying to do, you know to get ready for finals and all, but maybe," she said politely, but somehow it kind of felt like she was blowing me off. I mean, I'm no perfect student, but not even Aiden, who is Mr. Honor Roll, spends Thanksgiving break studying. Though I didn't expect to hear from her, we exchanged numbers anyway before I went to get my black tea latte and find Aiden.

I found him in the denim section at Macy's looking at a pair of way-too-expensive jeans.

"Dude, you are such a girl! What is taking you so long?" I asked, hoping to annoy him. I really was feeling awful and wanted desperately to go home.

"Stop rushing me. Go find yourself something decent to wear. I'm not the only one who's been wearing the same thing over and over. No wonder you haven't had a date yet."

If he only knew the truth. Thinking about Cade again made the pain in my gut intensify. Unable to stop myself, I doubled-over in pain, clutching my middle, and trying to keep tears from pouring out of my eyes. I looked up and saw that Aiden had dropped the jeans he was looking at and was approaching me quickly.

"Alli? What's wrong? Talk to me!"

"I think we need to go, okay? I'm sorry," I said weakly.

"Come on. I'll drive."

As Aiden drove us home, I closed my eyes and tried to wish the pain away.

Chapter 35

Kendall

I was checking my make-up in the mirror one last time before Cade arrived. It had to be flawless, now that I was back in his good graces. Mom walked up behind me and commented, "You need more lipstick. Maybe a bit more blush. You're looking a little pale."

I stared back at her in the mirror and fought back the urge to tell her that she was looking a bit old, and maybe she could use a bit of Botox. Instead, I said nothing and adjusted my makeup to her liking, knowing that it was the best way to get her off my back.

"Better," she said as she walked away, thankfully leaving me alone to finish getting ready.

Cade called last night and asked if he could drive me to school today. He said, and I quote, "I think we need some alone time." Alone time! It's been forever since we had any of that. Applying a final coat of lip gloss, I heard Cade pull into the driveway. I practically ran downstairs and into his arms.

"Hey, I've missed you," Cade admitted as he pulled me in for a tight hug.

He pulled back and smiled before he kissed my perfectly-glossed lips.

I gently rubbed the proof of our kiss off his lips before responding, "I missed you too, baby."

"So, how about we take your new car to school and I'll leave my bike here? I've never been in an X5 before."

Could he be any sweeter? I was actually totally bummed about not getting to drive my new Beamer today, but I wasn't going to pass up riding to school with Cade, especially since he finally seemed to be over the little mishap that happened with Allison.

Cade opened my door to let me inside, and as he walked around the back of the car, I pulled down the rear-view mirror to make sure I still looked great.

Of course, when he got in, he ooohed and ahhhed just like everyone else had. Just knowing I had the hottest car on the estate made me feel a little better about how the last few weeks had turned out. But none of that mattered, now that Cade was back with me and had officially dumped the hussy he'd been screwing around with. I hope he realizes just how lucky he is that I'm so forgiving!

"So, what do you think of my new baby?" I asked.

"I love it," he said as he messed with the satellite radio.

He leaned over and gave me one more quick peck before we took off. We were making our way onto the main road when I saw the only other new car on the estate. Knowing exactly who was driving the silver Jetta, I sped up and honked my horn.

I couldn't stop myself. I smiled at Alli, gave her a little wave, and sped past her new piece of shit.

I looked over at Cade and surprisingly, he didn't seem fazed. I half-expected him to scold me, but he didn't. He just kept messing with the radio like nothing had happened.

After a minute or so of silence, he looked up and said, "How about we stop and grab some coffee? We have some time to spare."

I gladly pulled into the Starbucks down the street from our school and since the drive thru was backed up, Cade offered to run in and grab us two mochas. I was sitting back listening to John Mayer when I got that strange sensation of being watched. I'm no stranger to being stared at, but I didn't like it when I didn't know who was doing the staring, so I sat up and glanced around expecting to find some creepy perv gawking at me.

It didn't take long to spot him. He must have come out of the donut shop down the road and was now standing about thirty feet from my car looking right at me. As soon as our eyes met, he winked at me, then immediately got in his car and drove off. Watching his car exit the parking lot, I realized who he was. Somehow I knew, without a doubt, he was the wolf from the woods. I'd remember those piercing blue eyes anywhere.

***

When Cade and I walked into the school together hand-in-hand, everything felt back to normal. Just the way things should be. Cade was mine again, and I wasn't letting him go without a fight ever again. I gave Cade a kiss before heading off to first period and said, "Bye baby! Save me a seat at lunch."

There was one thing that I needed to do before going to class. I needed to track down the little bimbo, Alli. We needed to come to an understanding. Luckily I didn't have to hunt long. Halfway down the main hallway, I saw Alli push her way into the girls' bathroom near the west wing.

When I pushed the door open, I caught Alli staring at herself. Our eyes met through the mirror for a quick moment before she leaned over and splashed some water on her face. To say that she looked like shit would be an understatement, but that didn't stop me from laying out some ground rules.

"God, Alli, at least put some bronzer on. You look dead," I said mostly just to be mean, but it was the truth.

"Go away, Kendall."

"Not yet. We need to talk. No, let me rephrase. I need to talk, and you need to listen and obey. Cade is off limits," I said.

That got the little slut-puppy's attention. She picked her head up out of the sink and just stood there staring at my reflection in the mirror.

"He has made his decision. If I see you looking at Cade, talking to Cade, or hell, if I even suspect that you are thinking about Cade, I will rip your ass apart. Do we understand each other?"

Alli reached over and grabbed some paper towels, wiped her face dry, and walked toward the door. She threw away her trash, opened the door, and turned to finally face me.

"I got it," was all she said before she walked out.

Chapter 36

Cade

Ever thought of jumping out of a moving vehicle? Yeah, me neither until this very moment. My fake smile and oh-yes-I'm-so-interested nods weren't going to last much longer if Kendall didn't shut the hell up about the stupid winter ball. We had been in the car for twenty-two minutes and thirty-nine seconds, and I wasn't sure how much more I could take.

"So for real, should I wear red or winter white? And don't say whichever! I mean it, Cade. This is super important," Kendall stressed.

Jesus Christ! Seriously?

I made sure my loving smile was intact and said, "I've always thought you looked sexy in red," knowing she would eat that up.

Kendall playfully slapped me on the arm, responding, "Oh babe, you're so sweet. That settles it then. Red it is."

Could she be any more self-absorbed? How did I ever put up with her? I could have killed her this morning when she waved at Alli. What a crazy bitch! Did she think that wouldn't bother me? That I would be all, *Hey Alli, look at me and Kendall riding to school together.*

All her blabbing wasn't helping my headache either. And why the hell did I have a headache anyway? I never had one before. Werewolves are not supposed to get sick, but I felt like crap since I woke up this morning. Hopefully, this was a one-day thing because I don't know how humans deal with this. Trying to block out Kendall's incessant blabbing, I found myself wondering if Excedrin would work on me.

"Cade! Are you listening to me?"

Ooops!

"Of course I'm listening."

"Then what did I just say?" Kendall demanded.

I had no idea what the hell she was going on and on about for the last five minutes. I tuned her out after she was pleased with my wear-the-red-dress answer.

I had to pull out the big guns on this one, so I smiled, winked, and said, "Did I mention how pretty you look today?"

"Oh Cade. I love you."

I swallowed the vomit coming up in my throat and rubbed her thigh.

"Say it Cade. I want to hear you say it too."

This was not happening! It felt wrong to say it even though I knew I didn't mean it. It was like I was cheating on Alli. It was crazy, but true.

"Cade, I'm waiting."

"Babe, you know I love you too," I lied.

"I know," she chirped.

And I tried to remind myself that they were only words.

Chapter 37

Allison

Day five of feeling like uber-shit. I went so far as to sneak off to the drugstore to buy some Dayquil, but apparently over-the-counter meds didn't work on half-weres. So I guess I was just supposed to suffer. If I didn't know better, I would think that I was suffering from morning sickness, but since you actually have to have sex to have morning sickness, I could rule that out.

I dragged myself out of bed, ran a brush through my hair, a toothbrush over my teeth, and fumbled down the stairs looking like death-warmed-over.

"Dude, Alli. You look like you're about to die. Are you sure you're okay?" Aiden asked when I reached the front door.

He rushed into the kitchen and handed me a Gatorade and a granola bar for the ride to school. Just the thought of food made my stomach turn.

I sipped the Gatorade on the way to school, and thankfully Aiden remained quiet most of the way there.

Somehow I made it to first period, but I was feeling worse by the minute. Maybe I should have just stayed home, but was trying to avoid Mom, knowing that she would freak out over me being sick. I've never really been sick before, but surely, it could happen, right? Especially since I was half-human. One thing was for sure, if I kept getting worse, I wouldn't be able to keep it from Mom for much longer. I already felt like I might keel-over at any moment.

I saw Teagan walk in, and I gave her a weak smile.

"Still feeling bad?" she asked.

"Yeah, but I'll survive."

"You sure? You might want to go see the nurse, just in case. You don't look so hot."

To get her to shut up as I really didn't feel like talking, I assured her, "If I don't feel better by lunch, I'll go see her. Besides, it's Friday and Thanksgiving break starts tomorrow, so I'm just gonna try to make it through the day."

"Just promise if you start feeling worse, you'll go."

I know she was just trying to be a good friend, but I was kind of tired of being told that I looked like shit. I was well aware of that. I felt like it too.

I dragged myself from class to class in a daze, laying my head down in each, but still trying to look attentive enough so that I didn't get in trouble.

At lunch, I sat with Teagan and tried to force down the granola bar that Aiden gave me to eat for breakfast. It wasn't making me feel any better. In fact, I quickly decided that it was definitely having the opposite effect. I tapped Teagan on the arm and said, "I'll be back, okay."

I never made it though.

***

I woke up to the nurse waving something under my nose. When I came to my senses, I noticed Teagan staring at me wide-eyed.

"Alli, are you okay? You passed clean out in the middle of the cafeteria," Teagan told me.

I tried to sit up, but the nurse convinced me to take it slow.

"Allison, I notified your brother. He is checking you out of school and will be here soon to take you home. Teagan, thank you for getting Alli here so quickly. You can head back to class now," the nurse said.

Teagan gave me a quick smile and told me to send her a text when I felt better, and then she left. The nurse brought me a small cup of Sprite and a few saltine crackers, but I wasn't ready for either of them quite yet. I assured her I would try to eat something as soon as I got home.

Just as I closed my eyes, Aiden came busting through the door. He walked right up to me and tried to pick me up.

"Aiden! Put me down. I can walk, you idiot. The last thing I need is for the whole school to see my brother carrying me out the door."

Aiden put me down and then looked around. "What's that smell? Do you smell that?" Aiden asked as his eyes searched the nurse's office for the source.

"Smell what?"

"I don't know. You sure you don't smell that? Never mind, let's get you home."

Chapter 38

Allison

"Do you think you have a fever?" Aiden asked as he reached across the seat to feel my forehead. I shooed his hand away and then really thought about his question. Yes, I thought I might have a fever. I never had a fever before. Mom said that my body temperature would run a little hotter than normal, but I doubt that this was what she meant.

"I'm fine. Just a little off. Leave me alone and drive," I said.

"But, you look really bad, and you're sweating like a pig. This can't be good. Mom told us that weres weren't supposed to get sick, Alli."

I didn't respond. I knew that he was right. I shouldn't be sick. I never even had a common cold. But what was I supposed to say? He was freaking out enough for the both of us. We sat in silence for a few minutes, and it was easy to see that the wheels were turning in Aiden's head. Surely, he would call Mom as soon as we got home, and then she'd freak out too. In no time we would probably be at Marcus's doorstep asking what we should do, and that was the last place I wanted to be. I was pretty sure that going to Cade's house wouldn't help my situation.

Without warning, the silence was broken. "You know, I heard Cade wasn't feeling so great either. Shari mentioned something about Kendall being all concerned about him."

I leaned my head back on the headrest and didn't bother to reply. I didn't want to talk about Cade. Cade sucked. And just the mention of his name made me feel worse.

"Omigod Alli! Do you think this could be some werewolf virus? It could happen, you know. Why couldn't it? There are those antibiotic resistant infections in humans. Why else would the two of you be sick at the same time all of a sudden?"

He had a point. Cade and I had shared plenty of germs, so I guess it would make sense, but surely we wouldn't be the only two werewolves to get sick.

"Of course, I wouldn't get sick. I probably can't even get sick, right? I'm like a learning-disabled werewolf," Aiden said with a pouty face.

I wanted to comfort him and tell him that he wasn't a "learning-disabled wolf", but I didn't have the energy to do that, or to tell him to shut up. Not while I was desperately trying to do three things at once: trying not to pass out, trying to look normal, and trying to think of what to say so that Aiden doesn't run inside and tell Mom that I have a freaky "werewolf virus."

"Hey Aiden, can we not tell the parents about what happened at school today? It's just embarrassing," I pleaded.

"What? Are you crazy? We have to tell Mom. Have you looked in a mirror lately? Look!" he said as he pulled the passenger side visor down, so I could see my pitiful reflection. I had to admit, it was pretty bad. My face was as white as a ghost, and the dark circles under my eyes made me look like I have just lost a boxing match. There was no way I could let Mom and Dad find out. I would never hear the end of it.

"Seriously, Aiden, I'm fine. Give me a day or two, and if I don't feel better, then I will tell Mom. I promise."

At first I thought that Aiden understood and that he would keep his mouth shut, for a while at least, but then he slammed his fist on the steering wheel and began to rant and rave.

"God damn-it, Alli! This could be freakin' serious. Cade is probably the strongest guy in the pack, and according to Shari, he looks like shit. And you… Alli, I'm sorry, but I've never seen you look this bad."

I just sat there. Nothing that I could have said would have calmed Aiden down. He was on one of his rolls, and it was best just to let him tire himself out.

"I know that you don't want Mom and Dad to know, but that seems a little selfish to me. I mean what if it spreads? What if Mom and Dad get it? What if you die? I would never be able to live with myself knowing that I should have said something. This could really be some serious shit, Alli!"

Finally he shut up, and the rest of the ride home was peacefully silent.

As soon as we pulled into our driveway, I eased myself out of the car and slowly made my way up to my room. I expected Aiden to dart inside and tell Mom that I was infected with the mysterious were-virus, but he didn't. Maybe he had thought about what I told him in the car and decided to wait. Since I didn't need to deal with a freaked-out mother, I gladly opened my bedroom door, lay down on my bed, and passed out before I even hit the pillow.

***

"Alli, baby, wake up. Come on Alli, we need to talk," I thought I heard Mom say, but I was just so tired that I couldn't be sure.

"Alli, I am really worried about you honey. Wake up and talk to me."

I opened my eyes and saw my mom sitting on the side of my bed. It was at that moment that I realized that I was soaked with sweat. Obviously, I was getting worse by the hour, and now there was no avoiding telling Mom what was going on. Especially now, that I was dripping with sweat and shivering like I was caught in a blizzard. Even I had to admit that this didn't look good.

"Alli, look at me."

I gazed up at her, trying my best to look as if I wasn't on my deathbed.

"Oh baby, come here."

She gathered me in her arms like I was six again, consoling me after I took a tumble off my bike and scraped my knee. She hugged me tight and then pulled back, placing her hands on my cheeks to get a good look at me.

"I know this must be horrible. You've never felt sick a day in your life, and I hate to see you like this. I wish I could make you feel better."

"What's wrong with me, Mom?" I moaned.

She took a few seconds and then inhaled deeply.

"Honestly, I can only think of one logical reason why you would be feeling like this. But it doesn't really make much sense. Maybe I should call your grandmother."

"No, Mom. Please don't get Gram involved. Just tell me what you think is going on."

"Well, I've only heard about it. There should be only one reason why a werewolf would fall ill like this, and it rarely happens these days."

She stopped talking again and looked off toward the window like she was trying figure out exactly what to say.

"Honey, have you been seeing anyone?" she questioned.

"What do you mean?"

"I know this is not what you want to be discussing with your mom, but this is important. Have you been romantically involved with someone on the estate because if you have, it's important that you tell me?"

I pulled the covers over my head. This can't be happening! What could seeing Cade possibly have to do with me being sick? Cade was going to hate me even more if I told my mom. Shit shit shit!

My mom pulled the blanket off my head, and I couldn't hide the tears rolling down my cheeks. I didn't even have the energy to try to wipe them away.

"Ahh, baby. It's okay."

"No it's not, Mom. It's not," I continued to cry in spite of myself.

"Why are you crying? Baby, you need to talk to me. We can figure this out."

By this time I sounded like a hysterical child as I sobbed, "But, he doesn't want to be with me anymore, Mom. He doesn't want me."

"Who baby? Who doesn't want you?"

"Cade."

"Oh shit, Alli," my mom said dropping my hand.

"I told you."

Mom just sat there, staring at the window again, seeming a bit lost for words.

After an extremely long, extremely uncomfortable moment of silence, I asked my mom for a few minutes alone to calm myself down. Without argument, she saw herself out telling me to let her know when

I was ready to talk. Something told me she needed some time to herself as well.

I managed to make it to the bathroom to blow my nose and get a cold rag to wipe my face. Shaky and a little unstable, I walked back to my bed to lie down. I don't know how long I was lying there alone in my room before my mom came back in, but it must have been a while because Mom was wearing her pajamas and she had a cup of hot tea with her.

"Are you ready to talk again, Alli?" Mom asked as she settled herself on my bed.

She looked nervous, almost as nervous as the day when she revealed her secret past to Aiden and me. I knew that I wouldn't like to hear what she was going to say. *You can't be with Cade. Cade can't love you. You and Cade will never work.* I had heard it all in my own head, but I just couldn't make my heart accept it.

"I feel broken Mom. I know it's stupid. I have only known Cade a little while, but Mom, I don't feel right without him." I barely finished my sentence when my mom reached over and took my hand.

"I won't say that I understand. I don't, but from what I have heard from you and the little your brother was able to tell me, it sounds like Cade may be your mate."

I didn't know what to make of that. I didn't even know what that meant. We definitely haven't "mated," at least in the only sense of the word that I knew.

"Finding a true mate is a very, very rare event these days. I remember hearing stories about members of our pack finding their mates, but the last mated pair that I know of is your great grandparents. They were the perfect pair, so loving, and caring, and considerate of each other. I remember that they were always smiling and finding ways to touch each other, even if it was just a little tap on the arm."

"Mom, that sounds really sweet, but Cade and I are not that. He doesn't want me remember," I reminded her.

"I really don't think that is the case. If Cade is your true mate, there is no way for him not to want you. We will figure this out Alli," Mom said as she stood and started to walk out of my room.

"Just try and get some rest, baby. We will talk more later."

Chapter 39

Cade

My phone rang, waking me from a much-needed evening nap. I would have let it ring, but when Allison's home number popped up on the screen, I had to answer it. "Hello?"

"Cade, this is Lillian, Allison's mother. Can we talk for a bit?"

Oh shit. I cleared my voice, trying to make myself sound as if I didn't feel like I was going to pass out at any moment.

"Hi, Mrs. Wright. Is everything okay with Allison?"

"Actually no. Cade, if you don't mind me asking, how are you feeling?"

"Um... Okay I guess."

"You haven't been feeling ill?" she questioned.

Okay this was weird.

"Well, yeah, I guess I have been feeling a little off lately. Why?"

She paused for a few seconds before she continued. "Cade, I really need you to be honest with me here."

"Okay... I've had a killer headache and been dizzy and nauseous. And..."

"No, no, no. I mean honest about what's been going on with my daughter," she said, sounding like a no-nonsense mom.

"Mrs. Wright, I'm not sure what to say. What's really going on here?"

"Well Cade, she's sick. Really sick, and as far as I can tell there is only one logical reason why she looks like she has the swine flu."

I had no idea what the hell she was talking about, but this conversation couldn't get any more bizarre. I didn't even notice that Alli was sick. What did it mean that Alli and I were both sick at the same time?

When I didn't reply, Mrs. Wright said, "I believe that you are my daughter's true mate."

WTF! I didn't even think that happened anymore. She couldn't be my mate, could she?

"Are you sure, I mean we never... you know? I mean, I never even considered that," I admitted, a little scared and a little excited at the possibility.

"I'm not sure of anything yet, Cade, but there is a way to find out for sure. Can you come over to the house? I think that you and Allison need to talk."

"I'm on my way. Mrs. Wright, can we not tell my father about this yet?"

"I think that would be for the best for now, but if you are mates, he will have to know eventually."

***

I was in such a hurry to get to Allison that I threw on the first pair of jeans, t-shirt, and boots that I saw, grabbed a coat that I wasn't even sure was mine, and ran out the door without bothering to tell anyone that I was leaving.

As I walked up to her door, my hands were shaking, probably from the cold, and surely because I felt like crap, but mostly because of the uncertainty of what was to come.

Chapter 40

Allison

I was startled out of an almost-asleep state when our doorbell rang. I heard Mom call for the visitor to come on in and that's when I heard the last voice I ever expected to hear. Without hesitation, I jumped off my bed and ran into the bathroom. One look in the mirror told me that Elizabeth Arden herself could not help me look less like the walking dead. So I just washed my face and quickly brushed my teeth and hair.

Nervously, I opened my door afraid that Cade would be in my room, and at the same time, afraid that he wouldn't be. Hearing his voice made my skin start to tingle and my heart race. I didn't know why Cade had this effect on me, but he did. I should have been furious with him for refusing to see the truth; that we belonged together, but as much as I would have loved to march downstairs and tell him to go to hell, the part of me that just wanted to wrap my arms around him and bury my face in his neck was much, much stronger.

"Allison, honey, can you come down?" my mom yelled from the bottom of the stairs.

"Just a sec," I called back hoping that my voice wouldn't catch and reveal just how anxious I was.

As soon as I began to make my way down the stairs, the intoxicating scent of Cade filled my head, my body, and unfortunately for me, my heart. Maybe Mom and Dad will let me move back to Houston, just until I graduate. Then I can go to some small college where no one knows me, and I won't have to suffer from seeing Cade and not being able to be with him.

My wishful thoughts fled the moment I saw his face. He looked... well, he looked unhappy and tired. I had never seen Cade so disheveled. His clothes were wrinkled, his hair was a mess, and the dark circles under his eyes almost matched mine.

"Hey Alli, why don't you two come have a seat," Mom suggested.

Timidly, I walked to the edge of the sofa and sat down without saying a word to anyone. I tried not to look at Cade. I knew that if I did, I would completely lose it and probably start sobbing like a psychotic fool.

"Cade, I don't know how much you know about true mates. It's very rare these days, so no one really talks about it anymore, but it does still happen," my mom explained.

"Can one of you fill me in on the whole mate thing? Since I only just heard of the term like five minutes ago."

Mom turned to me and gave me a little head-tilt-smile combo like I was a five-year-old who just asked how babies are born.

"Come on Mom, I just found out that werewolves were real a few months ago. I know you are not very good at it, but can you just be straight with me."

To my surprise, it was Cade who spoke up first.

"True mates are like…" Apparently, he was having trouble finding the right words as well, which made me even more nervous.

After a few seconds, my mom cut in. "Alli, it's just kind of hard to explain. I guess the closest thing to it would be what you would think of as soul mates. Two people that are meant to be together. Except with weres it's a little more complicated. True mates are not just meant to be together. They *have* to be together. They are mated for life, and one of the signs of being mated is that you become ill if you are kept apart for too long. It's a chemical thing. Actually, I hate to admit that I haven't noticed until now, but your scent has changed a little, Alli."

Mom was quiet for a while, probably letting it all sink in.

"So, what does this mean for me and Alli?" Cade asked seeming genuinely concerned.

"I just mean that my father… he just would never allow this. He has forbid me from spending time with Alli," Cade said.

"What! You didn't tell me that," I practically yelled at Cade.

Cade moved closer to me and took both of my hands in his, "I'm sorry… I'm sorry I didn't tell you. I was scared that… I don't know what I was scared of. He made me promise to stay away from you. He told me that it was my duty to the pack to work things out with Kendall. He's my alpha and my father. I didn't know what else to do, Alli. I should have been honest with you."

"I think you two need to take a walk, get some air. I bet you will start to feel better soon," Mom suggested. "But don't go too far, it looks like a storm is coming."

With Cade sitting so close and his warm hands in mine, I almost didn't hear what my mom said over the sound of my own heart racing. It wasn't until Cade stood that I snapped back into reality, grabbed my coat, and walked out into the evening.

Chapter 41

Kendall

On my way over to Shari's, I saw Cade headed in the direction to Allison's house. He'd been acting strange all day. Pretending he didn't feel well.

I kept my distance, but followed him to his destination, and my suspicions were right. He went straight up to Allison's front door.

I waited, needing to see how long he would be there, and if he and Allison would leave together. It wasn't too long before her door opened again, and I watched as Cade and Allison walked out together. They headed toward the lake, so I did what any self-respecting girl would do. I followed them.

***

Through the trees, I could see the no good, two-timing bastard and his little mistress heading toward their favorite make-out spot, the pier. Forced to keep my distance so that Cade wouldn't sense my presence, I couldn't hear what they were saying, even in my wolf form. But from the looks of things, Cade was going to have some serious explaining to do.

Hand-in-hand, they walked along the water's edge, and I prowled along behind them, unable to believe what I was seeing.

What the hell was he thinking? I had half a mind to head over to the alpha and tell him myself, but not until I knew for sure what I was up against. Obviously, that little mutt was up to something. There was no way Cade would openly defy his father like this without someone whispering in his ear. He knew what his father was capable of. There was no way that prick had the balls to disobey the alpha, not without good reason.

Out of nowhere, Cade stopped walking and pulled the skank toward him. I almost vomited in my mouth. Even from where I was standing, I could see the longing in her eyes. She was so pathetic. I was still too far away to hear what Cade was saying, so I circled around to try to get a closer look without being seen. That was when I saw the strange wolf again. What was he doing? Was he following me or Cade? Either way, it needed to stop.

I decided that I had seen enough of the love-sick pups. It was time to find out who the creepy wolf was and what he was up to. I turned and walked toward him. Surprisingly, he didn't run. He stood there and waited for me to approach him. I came within a few feet of him; he didn't smell like a threat, so I motioned him to follow me. And he did.

Chapter 42

Allison

Walking around the lake, hand-in-hand with Cade, felt like forever since we had been together. It's funny how fast your life can change. This morning, I was completely miserable and felt like I had been in the octagon with a world-champion cage fighter, this afternoon I passed clean out in the cafeteria, and now… now I was starting to think that this could just be the best day of my life. I needed to remember to give my mom a huge hug when I got home, since she was the reason Cade came over tonight. The farther we walked, the better I began to feel. I guess being near Cade was just what the doctor ordered, and I guess now I knew why.

Cade and I may have been wandering in a comfortable silence through the estate, but my mind was on over-drive. True mates… what did that really mean? Together forever? Would he really always be mine? Obviously we couldn't stay apart, but did that mean we would have to spend the next eighty years attached at the hip or risk looking like victims of Aiden's werewolf virus.

Out of the blue, I felt the warmth of Cade's breath in my ear as he whispered, "What's going on in that beautiful head of yours?"

The way the mere sound of his voice sent tingles down my spine, the way his warmth seeped its way inside me, made it difficult to walk and talk at the same time. My feet stopped on their own accord as I look up into his eyes, "I don't know, Cade. I just can't believe this is all happening."

He wrapped his arms around me and pulled me into a hug. "Me neither, Alli… me neither."

"Where does this leave us? There's Kendall… and your dad. What is everyone going to say?" I asked.

"At this point, there is nothing anyone can say. Not even the elders of our pack would interfere with a mated pair. True mates are rare and their bond is sacred… our bond is sacred," he added just before he pressed his lips to my forehead.

We continued walking farther and farther from my house, both seemingly lost in our own thoughts and feelings, when the first drop of icy rain fell. It took only seconds for the heavens to completely open up and we were drenched. Cade grabbed my arm and began to run, "Hurry! We aren't too far from the old hunting cabin."

By the time we made it inside the cabin, I was literally shaking, not to mention dripping rain water all over the tiled floor. But all I could do was stand there and shiver. My brain and frozen body didn't seem to be cooperating. Thankfully, Cade could think and move, or we would have surely frozen to death right there.

Cade went straight to the linen closet and grabbed a few towels, and to my surprise two fluffy, pink robes. He handed me one of each and pointed toward the bathroom. I smiled, thinking how weird it was to have girlie, pink robes in a very manly hunting lodge. Cade saw my smirk and said, "My mom makes us keep these here for the women in the pack."

No matter how frosty I was I couldn't help but jest, "Uh huh, likely story."

With a gentle shove toward the restroom, Cade said, "Shut up and go get warm before you get frostbite!"

***

I walked out of the bathroom in my big comfy robe, feeling a little less like a Popsicle, only to find Cade bent over the fireplace with his pink, fluffy butt in the air. A very girlish giggle escaped before I could stop it. Not missing a beat, Cade turned toward me and began to model his new look.

"Uh-huh, you think this is quite comical, don't you, Alli? Never thought I could pull off pink? Well, I guess I will have to prove it to you." My hand flew up to my mouth, and I couldn't stop giggling if I tried as he danced around the room in what could only be described as part Demi Moore from Striptease, and part 1985 Miss America jazz routine. It was kind of funny and kind of hot at the same time.

Imagine my surprise as Mr. Serious himself began parading around like an old-school burlesque dancer, showing just a little and then taking it back. I didn't know whether to laugh or grab him by the pink, fuzzy robe, and kiss him until my lips hurt. He wiggled and giggled himself my way and tried to grab my hand, but there was no way I was taking part in his little version of Soul Train.

"Come on Alli, dance with me!" he said as he shimmied around in front of me.

"No way. You're doing a great job though. Really, keep it up," I told him still laughing.

He took my hand, spun me around, and wrapped his arms around me forcing me to sway with him to the imaginary music. I decided, well, screw it. If he was willing to act like a fool, who was I not to join in?

I wrenched myself out of his grip and danced around just out of his reach. Every time he took a step toward me, I took one back. I should have known better than to start a game like this, cat-n-mouse with a werewolf? Already, things weren't looking so good for the mouse. I saw that glint in his eyes just before he attacked. Before I knew it, I was pinned to the couch and Cade was staring down at me.

It was at that moment that I realized just how little we both had on. And the look in Cade's eyes had changed; we weren't playing anymore. Time slowed as he leaned down and brushed his lips across mine. He took his time kissing me, exploring my mouth, until he deserted my lips to nibble on my neck. I didn't have time to think or even to doubt what we were doing, because as he made his way back to my lips the kisses changed.

Suddenly, our kisses were urgent, desperate, necessary. Cade was like the oxygen that I needed to live. My hands had a mind of their own. They ran up his tight chest and pulled the silly, pink robe off his shoulders. I wanted... needed to feel his skin on my skin. I felt him hesitate and pull back a little.

"No Cade, don't stop," I whispered as I pulled him back to me. I wanted this. I wanted him.

Chapter 43

Kendall

Walking out my back door, now fully dressed, I hoped that the wolf would still be waiting. He did follow me home through the storm, so I could only assume that he must have wanted to chat, though I couldn't for the life of me figure why. Since he's been lurking about for some time now, there must be a reason for his sudden appearance on our land. While weres are generally always welcome on the estate, it's not customary for outsiders to show up without introduction from the alpha.

It was then that it occurred to me that he might be the "dangerous" wolf that Marcus had warned us about. Why hadn't I thought of that before? Before I motioned for him to follow me home. I could only hope that he wasn't as dangerous as our pack leader assumed.

Standing on my front porch, it didn't take long to find him standing only a few feet away, near the side of my house, no longer in wolf form. "For the love of God, cover yourself," I said as I threw the human stranger a towel. Apparently this guy had no shame. It didn't seem to bother him in the least that he was standing there in the dark completely naked. He sure took his time drying off and wrapping the towel around himself.

He walked up onto the porch with a sly grin on his face, but didn't speak, so I asked, "So what's up with you? You've been prowling around the estate for a while now. Does Marcus even know you're here?"

Now standing only a few feet away, he held out his hand and answered, "My name's Dylan, Dylan Christianson. Nice to finally meet you, Kendall."

His ice-blue eyes sparkled under a set of full, dark brows. He would have been considered handsome if it wasn't for the nasty scar that ran from his right cheekbone to the edge of his thin, firm lips. The scar made him seem dangerous, kind of dirty-hot. Not my type, but hot none-the-less.

"Why are you following me?" I asked.

"Because you told me to," he replied in a sexy, husky voice.

Any other girl probably would have melted just from the subtle hint of flirtation in his voice, but I'm not just any girl. He'd have to work a little harder than that to make me melt.

"Not now. I have seen you watching me before today." When he didn't respond, I asked, "Are you the rogue that our Alpha warned us about?"

"On that, I'm pleading the fifth. And I hate to burst your bubble, but I'm not watching you. Don't get me wrong, you are definitely worth watching, but I have been following Cade, not you," he said closing the distance between us.

"Cade, why are you following him?"

"Just checking out my competition. I like to know what I'm up against," he said. Now he was confusing the hell out of me. Did he really mean what I think he did?

"Competition? What? You don't seriously think you have what it takes to be alpha of this pack, do you? The elders would eat you alive, not to mention Marcus. You probably wouldn't even be able to get your hands on Cade."

"It's not Cade I plan to get my hands on," he said cryptically as he moved in even closer.

He was now standing so close that I could actually feel the heat coming off of his perfectly ripped body, and... well, he was quickly beginning to change my mind about him not being my type.

He leaned down and I thought for a second that he was planning to kiss me. But he didn't. Instead, he whispered in my ear, "Don't worry, honey. I have big plans for you too." Then he handed me the towel and turned to walk out into the rain.

Chapter 44

Cade

"Alli, baby, wake up," I whispered as I ran my fingers through her silky, blonde hair. Without opening her eyes, she stirred just a bit, wrapped her arm around my waist, and cuddled up against me. It would have been so easy to just lie back down and drift off to sleep, but Alli's parents would worry. Not to mention the fact that when my dad finds out that I disobeyed his direct orders and that Alli and I are true mates, he was going to come unglued.

"Come on Alli we need to get back. Your mom is probably worried about you."

"Is the storm over?" she asked sleepily.

"Yeah, we really should head back. I have to talk to my dad," I said.

A distressed look came over her face, and it just about broke my heart. I leaned down and kissed her cheek.

Wrapping my arms around her, I pulled her closer, hoping to ease some of her tension. "It's going to be okay, baby. There is no one, not even my father, who can keep us apart now. We are mated," I said with a smile that I couldn't contain.

Looking up at me, Alli asked, "What do we do now?"

My life had never been more perfect and screwed up at the same time. Here I was with the one person that was made just for me. It may sound unbelievable, but it was true. She was now a part of me that I couldn't be without. Finding your true mate these days was practically unheard of, but here we were, and I knew it was the real thing.

Tonight was the single best night of my life. It wasn't just the sex either. Being with Alli was different. Something about her made me feel more... more aware, more alive. More like me, and not who everyone expected me to be.

What do we do now? I didn't have an answer for her. Only time would give us the answer to that. The one thing I did know for sure was that no one could keep us apart. Realizing that I didn't have an answer for her, Alli looked away, and I took the opportunity to slip my alpha ring off my finger without her seeing.

I could hardly stand to see the disappointment on her face after what we had shared together. I wanted to make it better... no, I *needed* to make it better. "Alli, look at me," I begged as I pulled her a bit closer.

"I love you, Alli. I've never felt like this before, and I never what to lose you. Please don't let my father or pack politics come between us. I love you more than anything. You know that, right?"

Tears formed in her eyes as she stared at me like I have completely lost my mind. Then she pulled me into a hug and admitted in my ear, "I love you too, Cade."

"I want to give you something."

Alli pulled away and asked, "What? What could you possibly have to give me?"

I opened her hand, knowing my ring would be far too large for her finger, and placed my alpha ring in her palm.

"Cade? Are you serious?"

I couldn't take my eyes off her. "Of course I'm serious. I want you to have it. Just put it in your pocket for now. But after we announce that we are true mates, I want you to wear it around your neck. Please, put it in your pocket."

As she tucked the ring away, I leaned down to kiss her perfect lips, the lips that were created just for me. She pressed her body against mine, and I suddenly wanted her all over again.

She pulled away for moment to say, "I think we can keep everyone waiting for a bit longer, don't you?"

***

We finally forced ourselves to leave the cabin, and as my house came into view, I felt tension building in my body. My insides seemed to have formed a Boy Scout knot, and out of nowhere, it became hard to breathe. Alli stopped walking and pulled me to a stop.

"Maybe you should do this alone," she suggested timidly.

I truly wanted Alli to come with me. I thought with her standing by my side, I would be a little braver, but I completely understood why she would be apprehensive. Who in their right mind would want to face my father and tell him that they went against his orders?

"You know, that's probably a good idea. Do you want to wait here so I can walk you home?" I asked.

"Sure," she said. She placed the palm of her hand on my cheek and wished me luck. I hesitated for a moment, not wanting to leave Alli, but even more than that, *really* not wanting to go and confront my dad.

She took a seat on our porch swing. I gave her one final kiss, said a quick, silent prayer, and walked through the front door.

"Where the hell have you been?" my father's voice boomed from the kitchen.

I hung up my coat and headed that way. I expected to find my dad in the kitchen ready to let me have it, but I wasn't expecting to see the worried look on my mother's face. As soon as I stepped into the room, my mom diverted her eyes to the floor, as if she couldn't stand to look at me. I felt horrible. I didn't mean to hurt anyone, or piss anybody off, for that matter. I did what I did because I had to, and I knew that I needed to be strong and hold my ground. I did nothing wrong and what I needed to say to my parents was too important to wait.

"I... I need to talk to you both," I said trying not to stumble over my words. I needed to sound confident, not like a little boy making excuses to his father for misbehaving.

"What is going on Cade? I'm not an idiot. It's quite obvious from the smell of you that you have been consorting with the Wright girl, though I expressly forbade you to be in contact with her," my father declared as he moved toward me like a madman.

I stepped back, both out of instinct and respect for his position. "I am sorry for disobeying you, but I am not sorry about being with Allison. It could not be avoided."

"Excuse me?" he barked as he looked at me like I had just slapped him in the face.

"Maybe we should do this in the morning, give everyone a chance to cool down," my mother suggested.

"No, Mom we have to talk now. Allison is outside waiting for me. I asked her to stay so I could walk her home," I replied.

I took a deep breath and continued, "I'm sure you noticed how sick I had been this past week."

"Sick? Cade, we don't get sick. You know that," Mom said.

Unbelievable! How could neither of them have noticed? Well, apparently, they hadn't. How sad was it that my own parents don't pay enough attention to realize that their only son, who "can't" get sick, was sick? Good to know.

When I didn't respond to my mom, Dad asked, "Why on earth would you think that you were sick?"

"Because I was, Dad. Fever, nausea, body aches; I thought I was dying. And then Mrs. Wright called me. I thought it was to yell at me for breaking things off with her daughter, but instead she asked me how I was feeling. When I told her that I felt ill, she asked me to come over. She asked me to come over because she *did* notice that her daughter was sick."

"What are you getting at Cade?" Dad interrupted.

The words flew out of my mouth before I could stop them. "We are true mates," I admitted.

"Bullshit!" Dad yelled.

"What? How can you be sure, honey?" my mother asked.

Dad turned his attention to Mom and protested, "Seriously, Noel. Tell me you aren't buying this crap! True mates? You have got to be kidding." He turned and faced me once more and continued his rant. "This is complete and utter bullshit, Cade! I can't believe you would think I would even entertain the idea that you and Lily's half-bred daughter are mates. She's not even really one of us."

I just stood there baffled, unable to find the words that I needed to respond to his tirade. I never thought of him as… what would it even be called? Prejudiced? Did he really believe that because Allison wasn't a full-blooded were that we couldn't be mates?

Mom placed her hand on my dad's shoulder and said, "Marcus! Please calm down. Insulting this girl is not helping matters."

"I'm not concerned about her feelings right now, Noel. I'm concerned about the future of this pack and the future of our only son."

"Allison is my future whether you like it or not, Dad," I yelled as I turned to leave the room and this conversation.

"We are not finished," Dad said as he grabbed my arm and forced me down into the chair next to my mother.

My father stood above us, only a foot or so away, but continued to shout just the same. "Cade, let's face the facts. Allison doesn't love you. She is only using you to raise her family's position in this pack. Lily screwed up all those years ago, and her family has never lived down the disgrace she brought on them. It's hard to believe that Lily would use her daughter to strengthen her family, but it is the only explanation. You're young Cade. You don't know what people are capable of and what they are willing to do for power. I'm sorry to be the one to tell you this, but Allison is just sleeping her way up the ladder, son."

I felt my fists clinch. I knew that I couldn't afford to lose my temper with the alpha, but to accuse Alli of sleeping her way to the top was asinine.

"If you are so worried about the future of this pack, you need to be careful what you say about my mate. You raised me to take over as alpha one day and that day is not far off. Allison will be by my side, so you're going to have to get used to it," I declared as I stood up, pushed passed him, and left the room.

My father started to say something, but I heard my mother, gentle as ever, ask him to leave me be.

I wanted to barge out of the house, grab Alli, and leave this place, but I couldn't let her see me this way. I needed a minute to calm down. Instead of walking out the front door, I darted up to my bathroom to splash some water on my face. A few minutes later, I went to get Alli, but when I walked out to the porch, she was gone.

Chapter 45

Allison

I could hear Marcus yelling at Cade on the other side the door, but it was difficult to understand exactly what he was saying. My curiosity obviously got the best of me since I found myself inching closer and closer to the door so I could hear what was going on. I knew it didn't sound good, but I was completely taken aback when I clearly heard Marcus shout, "…You're young Cade. You don't know what people are capable of and what they are willing to do for power. Allison is just sleeping her way up the ladder, son."

I backed up, unable to believe that anyone would think that of me and immediately felt blood rush to my face and tears welling up in my eyes. Thoughts of storming into their house and exploding on Marcus were running through my mind. Each scenario I thought up had one thing in common; they all ended badly for me and Cade, so before I did something I would later regret, I turned and walked away.

There was no way I could have stood there on that porch, waiting for Cade to come back out. Not with his family thinking that I was using their son to get to the top of the pack. I needed to get home, and as much as I would've loved to have Cade take me there, I needed to be alone. I couldn't face him; not after what his father said about me.

The walk from Cade's place to mine wasn't far, but it was long enough to make me feel desperately lonely. Halfway home, I wished that I had stayed and waited for Cade. I wished that I could have held my emotions in check so that I could have confronted Marcus and called him a liar to his face. I wished that Cade and I were still in the hunting lodge together and I hadn't heard his father's angry outburst, but none of that was going to happen.

The only good thing that came out of this whole debacle was that now I was completely convinced that Cade and I were true mates.

Almost immediately, after being near him, I had felt better. Healed, as if I had never been sick at all. And the way Cade looked at me, touched me, and held me in his arms, made me forget the world around us.

I didn't understand why Marcus didn't believe Cade and me to be true mates when it was so obviously true. You would think that finding a true mate would be something to be celebrated. Where was our balloons and cake? Where was our fucking piñata? No, instead, Cade gets yelled at, and I get called a slut. Somewhere in the middle of my internal rant, I realized how alone I was.

The forest can make some ominous noises when you're walking through it during the night all alone. It's like the woods are purposely trying to scare the hell out of you so that you never walk alone again. The tree branches cast the most frightening shadows, and the insects seemed to chirp in surround-sound.

As fear took hold of me, my steps quickened. To add to my paranoia, I could now hear heavy footsteps to my right, and I would have sworn that only a moment ago, they weren't there. I took a deep, bravery-building breath and looked in the direction of the noise, hoping to find Cade. But it wasn't Cade.

I saw a shadowy figure heading toward me. I saw a gun. That was the last thing I saw.

Chapter 46

Kendall

I couldn't sleep. How could I? Not after my little run in with that wanna-be alpha. Who did this Dylan Christianson dip-shit think he was? Did he really think he could just wander through and take over this pack?

I turned over on my side, trying to get comfortable, but there was just no way I was going to sleep anytime soon. I needed to talk to Cade. I couldn't let Dylan do this to our pack. If he really was determined to challenge Marcus and Cade, then that meant that my position was being challenged as well.

Cade and I might be on the outs now, but as soon as I could figure out how to get Alli out of the picture, it will be me and Cade running this pack together before too long. I got up out of bed and fumbled around in the dark trying to find the jeans that I had on earlier.

With my phone in hand, I took a few deep breaths, trying to decide the best course of action. I needed to tell someone. Just as I began to dial Cade's number, I heard a rustling in the bushes outside my window. Instinctively, I jumped up and headed toward the noise, but before I could pull back the curtains, there was a knock on my window.

Hesitantly, I pulled the drapes aside. "Hey, remember me?" Dylan said through the glass.

I pushed open my window and stared at the guy who had been keeping me up all night.

"Are you crazy? What are you doing here?" I asked.

"Come out here. I have a surprise to show you," he said with a wink.

I thought about shoving the window closed, calling Cade, and forgetting about any surprise Dylan might have, but that's not how I do things, so I grabbed my robe and boots, and headed outside.

With a flashlight in his hand, Dylan prowled toward his car, like a cat-burglar.

"What the hell is going on here, Dylan?" I asked as I followed him over to my driveway.

He turned in my direction and held the flashlight under his chin like he was preparing to tell a scary, campfire story, as he said, "You'll see."

"You really have lost your mind, haven't you?"

"Oh, you have no idea!" he admitted with a sly grin as he popped the trunk.

Holy mother of God!

"What the hell have you done?" I asked, staring down at the body of Allison Wright.

"Don't get your panties in a wad. She's not dead. Just resting peacefully."

Well, that was definitely better than dead.

"What is she doing in the trunk of your car?" I asked, slightly afraid to hear his answer.

"Technically, this is not my car. It's Gage's. I just borrowed it."

"Could you answer my freakin' question?"

This was absolutely unbelievable! I grabbed his flashlight and pointed it toward Allison, searching for any sign of life. She looked dead, and lying on a sheet of plastic with blood dripping from a cut on her head made things look all the worse.

"Well, if you must know, this is step one of my evil plan. Abduct the girl. You want to know what step two is?"

"I'm afraid to ask."

"I'll give you the condensed version. 1) Abduct the girl, 2) weaken Cade, 3) challenge Cade, 4) challenge Marcus, 5) make you my mate. So, what do you think? Oh, and 6) rule the pack."

"What do I think? I think you are a lunatic! I think you clearly have a death wish, and I don't want to have anything to do with this insane plan."

I turned and started walking away. "I'm calling Marcus. And you can't stop me. He needs to know what you are up to."

Dylan grabbed me by the arm and pulled me into a suffocating hug. "Calm down, sugar. My plan will work. Trust me."

"You do want to run this pack one day, don't you?" he asked.

"Of course I do."

"You do know that the only way that will ever happen is if you are with me, right?"

"What do you mean? Cade is not getting rid of me," I said.

"Oh honey, haven't you been paying attention? I certainly have. Alli here, is Cade's true mate. You're officially out of the picture... but if you want a way back in..."

True mate? No way! This couldn't be happening. I couldn't speak. Words were caught in my throat, and all I could do was take a step back, lean over, and rest my hands on my knees. My breathing was rushed, and my head was swimming.

I managed to look over at Dylan, who was standing there looking as smug as ever. He reached up to shut the trunk and said, "Oh come on, Kendall. Get a grip. You're tougher than that. You are supposed to be the alpha female of this pack. Are you really going to freak out instead of doing what needs to be done?"

I sat down as I concentrated on controlling my breathing. I pushed aside all of the built up anger, hurt, and betrayal. In its place came a need for revenge. I was not losing my place in my pack to anyone.

"So why take Alli? How is that going to help us?"

"Us, huh? I like that. The longer Alli and Cade are apart, the weaker they become. If we can keep them apart long enough, Cade will be as weak as a new pup."

"So what are you planning to do with her?" I asked as I pointed to the trunk.

"What happened to *we*?"

Oh no, no! Was he out of his mind? There was no way I was getting involved in this mess... anymore than I already was, anyway.

Dylan leaned against the trunk and said, "Come on Kendall. We can do this. This pack can be ours. Me and you. We can rule this pack together. Help me think of somewhere to stash the girl."

"Just leave her in there," I suggested.

"I don't think it's a good idea to keep her in a trunk for a week. We need something more private. Something close by, but deserted."

I thought about it for a minute before the perfect location dawned on me. "My mom has a ski cabin just outside the estate," I offered, though I could hardly believe that I was getting caught up in Dylan's take-over-the-pack plan.

"Perfect. I knew I could count on you," Dylan said before he lightly kissed my cheek.

Chapter 47

Allison

I woke to the sound of two voices. One I immediately knew to be Kendall's. The other sounded vaguely familiar, but I couldn't place where I had heard it. It was a male voice, and it only took a moment of eavesdropping to determine that he was the mastermind behind my abduction.

I was lying on a bed with my hands and feet tied, and one killer headache. Luckily, they didn't see me open my eyes, and I had enough wits about me to shut them again before they realized that I had regained consciousness. With my eyes closed, I listened intently to their scheming.

Kendall: How long should it take?

Male voice: I'm guessing about a week.

Kendall: You're guessing. You mean you don't know. Jesus, Dylan.

Ah ha! The mystery voice belonged to the asshole in the woods.

Dylan: A week should be enough time for Cade to weaken.

Kendall: Why can't you just get rid of her?

Dylan: Seriously? You are ready to just up and kill her? Besides, if we kill her, their bond will be broken. Cade won't weaken at all, and we will be left with one angry son-of-an-alpha. We can't kill her... yet.

Kendall: So what are we going to do with her for a week?

Dylan: Well, you have to go back to the pack, so you can keep me updated as to what is going on and so nobody gets suspicious. I guess while you're gone, I'll stay here and take care of our little friend in there. I did see a Wii around here, didn't I? I might just have to pass the time playing *Madden*.

Kendall: Uh-huh. Great plan. I hope you know what you are doing.

Dylan: Don't worry. It will all work out. After a week or so, I'll take care of Cade, and then I'll let you take care of our little friend on the bed here. After that, it will be easy to take out Marcus. You'll see. This pack will be ours.

Kendall: So what now? I just head back and act like nothing has happened?

Dylan: Exactly. Text me soon.

After saying goodbye, Kendall walked out the door, and just like Dylan said, he started up the Wii.

I had to get the hell out of here. I squeezed my eyes shut, tried to concentrate, and pictured myself in wolf form, but all that followed was excruciating pain behind my eyes. It took everything I had not to scream out in agony.

I tried to slow my breathing and relax. I can do this. I had done it before. Changing was my only way out of these ropes. Breathing deeply, I closed my eyes and tried again. But before I could even focus, the pain was back and worse this time.

Exhausted, I surrendered, deciding that changing wasn't an option. Instead, I watched the douche-bag play Madden for almost an hour before I finally decided to speak. He hadn't even bothered to look my way. I could have had a concussion or something, but apparently, he wasn't too concerned.

I cleared my voice and said, "I need to pee."

"Oh, you're awake. Good. We have so much to catch up on," he said, as he paused his game and put the controller down.

"Can I go to the bathroom first?"

"Sure honey," he said as he leaned over and untied my legs.

It felt good to finally stand up and stretch a little. I looked around the room and then at him. He finally realized what I was looking for and said, "Right there to the left."

I walked into the restroom and turned around to shut the door, but Dylan was standing in the way.

"Afraid not, honey. Don't worry, it's not the first time I have seen a girl pee before."

Oh fabulous. He actually expected me to use the restroom in front of him? Thankfully, he made a production by putting his fingers in his ears and whistling at the shower curtain. It was quite a feat getting my jeans down and then back up with my hands still tied together.

On the way back to the master bedroom, Dylan apparently decided that he needed to fill me in on his evil plan, which wasn't exactly the same evil plan that I had overheard. This version didn't include killing anyone, especially me. According to him, I had nothing to fear. Supposedly, I would only be inconvenienced for a week or so, and then I would be set free to return to the pack. Little did he know I knew the truth.

When we entered the bedroom, he motioned toward the bed, and said, "Get comfy. I have a game to finish."

Chapter 48

Cade

After realizing that Allison had left my house, I ran directly to her place hoping to explain away my father's assholishness. But she wasn't there, and immediately, my search began. Now it was two o'clock in the morning, and I have been to her house, our swing, the cabin, and back to her home again. It was time to ring the doorbell.

The light was on in the kitchen, so I hoped that someone was still awake. It didn't take long for Mrs. Wright to answer the door, and it was obvious that she was worried too.

"Oh my God, Cade. Do you know what time it is?" She looked around and asked, "Where's Allison?" her tone immediately shifting from irritation to panic. Seeing me shivering, she grabbed my arm and ushered me inside.

I stood there not knowing how to answer without making things worse, so I just told her the truth. "I don't know. I was hoping she was here."

"What? I thought she was with you," she said as she led me to a chair in the kitchen.

"She was. We went to my house to tell my dad about us. I asked Allison to let me go in by myself first, but she must have heard my dad shouting at me from where she sat on the porch. He didn't take the news very well. When I made it back outside, she was gone."

Mrs. Wright poured me a cup of coffee and leaned against the counter looking outraged.

"I have looked for her at every place I could think of. I have to find her and explain. My father said some horrible things," I admitted.

"I tried to call her a few times, but it just went to voicemail. What exactly did Marcus say that would have caused her to run off like that?" Mrs. Wright asked.

At first, I had no intention of repeating what my father had said, especially not to Alli's mother, but I knew that she deserved to know. After she heard the abridged version of the argument, she proceeded to explode. She called my dad every dirty word in the book, woke up the whole house, and only moments later, she was on the phone with her mother, a council elder.

"Cade, bro, what are you doing here?" Aiden said as he walked into the kitchen to see what was going on. When no one answered, Aiden asked, "What has my sister done now?"

Chapter 49

Kendall

It had been seventeen hours since Allison went "missing," and the entire pack was called in for an emergency meeting at the Lodge. All I had to do was keep my cool and report anything important back to Dylan.

I walked into the Lodge with Shari and Becca, and we took our usual seats near the back. I noticed Alli's parents standing in the front of the room with some of the council elders. They both looked so panicked that I almost felt bad for them. Almost.

Shari elbowed me and whispered, "Hey, look over there. What's wrong with Cade?"

I looked over and saw Cade sitting next to Aiden with his head in his hands. The tiny part of me that felt guilty for what Dylan and I had done vanished. Cade deserved to suffer.

On one hand, I knew that he couldn't help who his true mate was, but on the other, I couldn't just sit there and watch someone else run this pack. This is my future, and it was time to look out for number one.

Marcus called the meeting to order, and everyone quickly found themselves a place to sit. Only seconds later, silence filled the room, and Marcus adjusted the microphone, but instead of beginning his speech, he moved aside for Allison's grandmother to take the podium.

Katherine Grant cleared her throat and spoke, "Fellow pack members, I want to get right down to business. I have some disturbing news to report. Allison Wright, my granddaughter, has gone missing."

Immediately, chatter spread like wild fire through the room, but when Katherine began speaking again, everyone quieted.

"She has been missing for just over seventeen hours now, and at this point, we have no leads as to her whereabouts. The council has come to an agreement on how best to handle the situation, and we are asking everyone to give us their full cooperation until she is found."

"Omigod! Did you know about this? Poor Alli," Shari said looking shocked.

"Of course I didn't know about this. I totally would have told you," I replied, hoping she couldn't see right through me. I gave a cursory glance around the room to make sure that no one was looking at me. I hadn't thought about it until just then, but I was the only person that Alli had problems with since the Wrights arrived. Surely, no one here would think that I was capable of kidnapping.

Katherine continued, "The council has agreed to wait until the estate has been thoroughly searched before we contact the local authorities. We are calling for an immediate, mandatory curfew following this meeting. During that time, every home will be searched by one of our search teams."

That was completely crazy! I didn't want people snooping around my bedroom. Apparently, I wasn't the only one who felt that way. The pack seemed to erupt in disagreement. Katherine's voice was drowned out by the crowd. Finally, Marcus stood and demanded their attention.

"This isn't an option nor shall it be discussed. You will cooperate. You will let the search parties into your homes. If this were your son, daughter, brother, or sister, you would want the same done for your family."

I couldn't believe my eyes when I saw my own mother stand up and call out over the crowd, "Marcus, this is ludicrous. Are you really accusing one of us? This is not only an invasion of privacy, but the fact that you actually suspect that one of us has anything to do with this is unbelievable. What is it about this girl that would cause you to show such distrust in your own pack?"

Marcus stood there for a moment before Katherine said to him, "Marcus, you need to tell them."

"Alright, the fact is that Allison Wright is my son's true mate."

That was all it took for the entire room to explode into conversation.

"Kendall, omigod! Are you okay?" Shari asked, her face full of pity.

At that point, I didn't know what to do. It didn't occur to me that the entire room would suddenly turn and stare at me to see my reaction to the news. I did the first thing that came to my mind. I jumped up from my chair and ran out of the Lodge pretending to sob. I figured that Becca and Shari would follow me, but I didn't stop running. I needed to get the hell out of there.

Chapter 50

Allison

I have been sitting here, watching this asshat play Madden all freakin' day. And to make matters worse, he really sucked at it. I could totally kick his ass, and I had only played it with Aiden a few times. The most annoying part was that every few minutes, he would ask, "Hey, did you see that play?"

I almost would rather he just killed me now and end this horrible suffering. If I could just figure out a way to get free, I could get out of here. Honestly, he seemed too stupid to be able to stop me. All I needed to do was change. It sounded so easy, but since my last attempt, I had been too afraid. Since that wasn't going to happen, I decided to try plan B.

Before he started his next game, I asked, "Hey, can I play? I'm bored, and I'll behave. Promise." Then I smiled innocently, hoping that if he was a big enough moron to untie me, I would have a chance to run.

"Seriously? You want me to untie you?" Dylan asked.

"I won't try anything. Honest. I'm just sick of sitting here doing nothing. And my arms are starting to cramp. You don't really think that little ol' me could overpower you, do you?"

That comment seemed to do the trick.

Dylan shook his head and said, "Of course you couldn't. But... you can't tell Kendall, okay?"

I smiled in triumph. He really was a schmuck.

After making me promise once more that I wouldn't try to get away, Dylan put down the Wii controller and untied my hands. Thrilled to finally have them free, I sat up and stretched a bit.

"So, how about we bowl instead?" I asked, hoping if he said yes, I could convince him to untie my feet also.

"Seriously?"

"Yeah, bowling's fun."

"Bowling's gay."

I put on my best pouty face, hoping that he wouldn't be able to resist.

"Fine."

Reluctantly, Dylan put in the new game, walked to the bed, and bent down to untie my feet. Seizing the opportunity, I grabbed the lamp off the bedside table and smashed it against his head as hard as I possibly could. I had hoped that this would be my chance to make a great escape, but the bastard just shook it off. He stood up, touched the fresh cut on this forehead, and said, "Damn girl, why did you have to go and leave a mark? Kendall's gonna have my ass. And now I have to tie you up again."

I just sat there for a moment staring up at him. Finally I said, "Oops, sorry. I didn't mean to cut you." I had meant to knock his ass out. Guess he's tougher than I thought.

"Great. Now we can't play the game," he pouted.

He re-tied my hands and feet and went to the bathroom to get a bandage for his head. A few minutes later, he was back at the end of the bed playing Madden like nothing had happened.

Chapter 51

Cade

We were organized into two search parties to scour the estate. I volunteered to lead one of the teams, but was shot down immediately by my father. No big surprise there. He claimed that I was too "emotionally wrecked" to get the job done right. I did demand to be in the same party as Allison's family. It may sound ridiculous, but being near them, somehow made me feel a bit closer to her.

It was decided that we would search half of the estate tonight and the other half tomorrow morning. According to our "fearless leader," no stone was to be left unturned. I was eager to get going and see what we could find, though my gut told me that she was no longer on our property. For some reason, I had a feeling that if she were here, I would have been able to sense her presence. I tried to convince the elders that we needed to be looking elsewhere as well, but, again, the idea was dismissed.

As we walked out into the night to begin our hunt, Allison's mom stopped me to ask, "Cade, are you sure you are feeling up to this?"

"I have to help! I can't just sit around and do nothing."

"But, you don't look so good. Are you feeling okay?"

I hadn't stopped to think about how I was feeling. All I could think about was finding Allison. But now that Lily had asked, I did have a bit of a headache. However, she didn't need to know that. It would only add to her concern for her daughter. If I was already feeling bad, Allison must be as well.

I gave her the best reassuring smile that I could manage and said, "I'm fine, really. Just worried."

"I'm worried too, Cade. But we are going to find her. Let someone know if you start feeling ill. Okay? You look a little pale," she said.

"I will," I agreed with a small smile, and then I hurried to catch up with Aiden.

***

Midnight was quickly approaching and we had turned up with absolutely nothing. The disappointment hung in the air like a thick cloud of smoke. I was beginning to notice all the looks of absolute pity thrown in my direction from the older members of the pack. They must be ready to give up for the night. Luckily for me, Aiden suggested that we finish this side of the lake tonight and pick back up on the other side in the morning.

We only had two houses left, Shari's and Kendall's.

Shari's mom, of course, was the ultimate hostess. She's always been one of the more matronly members of our pack, and she must have known that we were near because she had a pot of hot coffee brewing and some fresh pastries waiting for us. As we headed to our last stop, I had a feeling that we might not receive such a welcome in the next home.

Man, I couldn't have been more right. Kendall's mom, Claire, was definitely not awaiting our arrival with home-baked goodies. She had the you-are-not-welcome-in-my-home look down pat. I hesitated at the front door, not sure if I should even step foot inside the Stuart home, but when Claire walked up to me and said, "Oh Cade, get in here. It is so good to see you. I'm afraid Kendall's not here right now, but you get in here out of the cold." I figured that everyone but me must be on her shit-list. Kind of unbelievable that she was still holding out that Kendall and I had a chance. She must think I'm a real fool if she thought that I didn't realize that was the only reason she was being nice to me.

After she dragged me safely inside, Claire gave the rest of the crew a stone-cold glare before she rattled off, "You know how unnecessary this all is? I can't believe Marcus is allowing this nonsense to go on. As if any one of us would be responsible for that girl's disappearance." Then, she had the nerve to turn her attention to Mrs. Wright and say,

"Did you ever consider that she ran away? You know a lot of unhappy teenagers run off. I bet she shows back up in a few days."

Mrs. Wright stopped what she was doing and replied, "You know Mrs. Stuart, this will only take a few minutes. Why don't you go have a seat, and we will be out of your hair shortly." And then she smiled smugly. It was clear that she wasn't going to let Claire get under her skin. It was hard to believe that she was holding it together as well as she was, under the circumstances.

Claire took the hint and surprisingly stayed out of the way while our team finished our search of their home and vehicles. Before we headed out, Mrs. Wright reminded Claire, "Mrs. Stuart, we were hoping that Kendall would be here, with the curfew and all. Please let us know when she gets home. We will need to search her car as well."

We were done with our search for the night, but there was no way in hell I could just go home and go to sleep. I wouldn't be able to get a good night's rest until Alli was back. On the way back to the Wright's house, I thought I picked up on Alli's scent. For some reason, I didn't tell anyone. Not yet. I wanted to check it out for myself. I thanked everyone for their help and quickly said my goodbyes. I didn't want to be rude, but I couldn't afford to lose her scent.

As soon as I was out of sight of the others, I transformed and dashed off into the night.

Chapter 52

Allison

I knew I couldn't have been asleep for more than ten minutes when the door opened and a blast of frigid, November air blew through the cabin, immediately sending chills deep down into my bones. Kendall came in already yelling up a storm about the "ridiculous search" that was going on at the estate. It made me feel a little better about the predicament I was in knowing that people were out searching for me. Kind of gave me a renewed sense of hope.

"Can you believe that they are actually going to search everyone's homes? And Cade is actually... holy shit, Dylan, what happened to your head?" she asked sounding genuinely concerned about the fresh cut on Dylan's forehead.

Dylan reached up and lightly touched the small gash as if he had forgotten it was there. Smiling sheepishly, he said, "Oh this? It's nothing. We just had a little accident."

With her hands now on her hips, Kendall said, "What do you mean we? What the hell was going on here while I was gone?"

Hoping to cause a rift in their little alliance, I admitted, "I convinced Dylan to untie me, and then I smashed a lamp over his head so that I could escape. If it makes you feel any better I didn't mean to cut him. I meant to knock him out. Anyway, it didn't work. He's tougher than he looks." Then I grinned and waited for the fireworks.

Kendall turned toward me, and I could literally see the rage building in her eyes.

"You, don't even speak to me," she yelled, and then turned to Dylan.

"Dylan, I am only going to say this once. You better open your god-damn ears and listen. If you untie that bitch one more time, I will gut you! You stupid dog. Jesus!"

Dylan just sat there completely shell-shocked. I think that for the first time since I've met him, he was speechless. He remained there a moment longer just looking at Kendall with eyes full of fury, then got up and left the room. Kendall shot me one more death glare before she followed him into the living room.

Even from the other room, I could hear their conversation thanks to my super-were ears.

"Kendall, I know that you are upset, and you have every right to be, but you will never talk to me like that again, understand? I'm not Cade. I'm not going to put up with that shit. Yeah, I'm the first to admit that untying Allison wasn't the smartest decision I have ever made, and I promise that it won't happen again, but I really thought she was harmless. Well, until she smashed my head in."

There was a moment of silence before Kendall apologized. I couldn't believe my ears! Kendall, stone-cold were-bitch, was admitting she was wrong.

"I'm sorry, Dylan. I just had a horrible day. Marcus announced to the entire pack, in front of all my friends, my family, my freaking crazy-ass mom, that Allison was Cade's true mate. I was mortified. Seriously, I wanted to die right there in front of everyone. They all turned and stared at me like I was some kind of freak. Dylan, I didn't know what to do, so I ran. I literally ran out of the Lodge. It was horrible," Kendall whined.

Marcus told everyone about me and Cade? Did that mean that he would accept our relationship? That he would allow Cade and me to be together?

Dylan changed his tone after Kendall's little breakdown. "Baby, come here. It will all be over soon. You don't need Cade. You have me now. And as soon as we get Cade and Marcus out of the picture, you will get back on top. Speaking of Cade, how did he look? Did he look sick, yet?" I heard Dylan ask.

Just hearing Cade's name made my head and my heart ache. If only I could find a way out of here. I looked around for like the hundredth time hoping to see something that I could use to escape. After my first failed attempt to flee, Dylan made sure that not only my arms and legs were tied together, but that I was tied to the bed as well.

I was just about to give up, when Kendall told Dylan that she thought their plan might really work out because the pack was only searching the estate. She said that Cade looked awful and that it served him right. Hearing that Cade was already feeling sick instantly made me panic.

I remembered Dylan saying that it would only take about a week for Cade to be sufficiently weakened, and I had no clue how long I have been here. I had to get out of here. I needed to help Cade, and I certainly didn't want to die in this stupid cabin. So, with no better option in mind, I started screaming for help and yanking on the ties so hard that my wrists began to bleed.

I saw Dylan and Kendall rushing toward me, but I didn't stop. With Dylan close enough to reach, I managed to kick him in the face with my tied-together feet. Again, the jackass didn't seem too fazed. Then, I saw Kendall coming at me with a syringe filled with God knows what. I thrashed about trying to stay out of her reach, but Kendall was able to hold me down, and the crazy bitch actually smiled when she jabbed the needle in my neck. Seconds later, my world went black.

Chapter 53

Kendall

I pulled into my driveway, turned off the engine, and sat in the car. I wasn't ready to go inside. I knew what I'd be forced to deal with once I opened the front door, and to be honest, it terrified me. An angry mother was one thing, but my mom took it to a whole other level. She will look at me with shame in her eyes, but only for a moment before she lays into me and tells me how this is all my fault. How I wasn't good enough, smart enough, pretty enough. How I wasn't strong enough.

I never have been.

Resisting the urge to pull out of my driveway and never look back, I gathered up my cell phone and purse and headed toward the front door. I took a few deep breaths and reminded myself that I could handle whatever she threw my way before I walked into my own little hell-on-earth.

She was waiting for me on the couch, drinking red wine. God only knew how many glasses of wine she had treated herself to before I wandered in. Not even bothering to look my direction, Mom asked, "So what did you do with the little tramp?"

Completely flabbergasted, I replied, "What?"

"Come on Kendall. I'm not an idiot, though I am quite surprised. I didn't think you had it in you. I just hope you don't screw this up like you do everything else."

Dropping my purse and keys on the console table near the door, I tried my best to appear innocent. "I don't know what you are talking about, Mom. Maybe you've had a bit too much to drink."

Comments like that always got her blood boiling, and as soon as it came out of my mouth, I knew it was a mistake. She put her half-empty wine glass down on the end-table and shot me her famous death-to-Kendall look.

"Mom, I didn't…"

"You didn't what dear? Mean to be a complete and utter bitch? Too late for that."

Her words slurred together a bit, which told me she was probably working on her third, maybe her fourth glass. She wasn't ready to hang her head in her soup just yet, but just buzzed enough to make this encounter as difficult as possible. If I'd waited another hour or so, she would have been passed out on the couch, and I wouldn't have had to deal with her.

"Kendall, I know you're involved in the Wright girl's disappearance, so just tell me, how are you planning on screwing this up even further? Obviously, you're too stupid to pull off something like this by yourself. I just hope your partner in crime knows what he is doing."

I didn't know what to say. Didn't know whether to confess or not. She'd most likely tell me what a dumbass I was and try to take over the whole situation. No, I couldn't tell her.

"Mom, I had nothing to do with it. I have no idea what happened to her," I lied, trying to ignore the fact that she could always see right through me.

Picking up her wine glass again, she smiled smugly and said, "Sure… I guess I should have known you didn't have the balls to take matters into your own hands. You're as worthless as your father."

I couldn't help but resent her. I wanted to hate her. But I didn't hate her. My heart betrayed me, as usual. I have spent my entire life trying to please her, and just once, it would be nice if she didn't look down on me; her worthless daughter, who couldn't do anything right.

I was groomed since birth to be the most beautiful, the strongest, the most popular; the girl most deserving of the future alpha's love. It never mattered to her what I wanted. It had never been about me; only about finding her way back to the top.

I didn't respond. I couldn't have found the right words to say anyway. Nothing I said was ever what she wanted to hear. Even when I tried my very best to be the daughter she expected me to be.

I turned away and headed for the kitchen, but she didn't hesitate to follow me.

"We weren't finished here, Kendall Avery Stuart."

Without looking in her direction, I said, "I don't want to talk about this, Mom. Allison is missing. This could be a good thing, you know. I could get him back."

Slamming her glass down on the counter, Mom slurred, "You better find a way to get him back. Whatever it takes Kendall. You know I am counting on you. We need this."

I wanted to tell her how desperate she looked. How pathetic she was sitting back guzzling wine when that was the very thing that got us into this mess. I wanted to tell her that she was an awful bitch for pressuring me to get with Cade all these years, just to raise her status in the pack. Just because she married for love, and it screwed everything up, shouldn't mean that I shouldn't have the chance to find someone to love; someone who would love me back.

Instead I said what she needed me to say. "I know Mom. I will figure this out."

If only Dad could have controlled his impulses. If only Mom hadn't tried to cover it up. I could have been living my life for me and not for her. But no. The sad truth was that my dad was a raging alcoholic who ended up "accidentally" killing a human, and my mom was so worried about her rank that she tried to sweep the incident under the rug. Now, Dad's gone and Mom's lucky she wasn't kicked out of the pack as well. And poor little me was barely old enough to walk when everything went to shit.

Now, it was left up to me to make things right.

I pulled a bottle of water from the fridge and told my mom goodnight. She didn't respond until I was almost out of earshot.

"You know, if you tricked him into knocking you up like I'd told you to, we wouldn't be in this mess."

I kept walking straight to my room. There was nothing more to say.

Chapter 54

Cade

I followed her scent through the woods and down the trail that led to the lake. I hated that her delicious scent was now tainted with the stench of fear. I should have never left her alone. I should have been able to protect her. I should have stood my ground with my father. But I didn't. It's my fault that she was scared and alone. In the distance, I could barely make out the pier, our pier. I ran closer to the edge of the water, trying desperately to find her.

Finally, I did find her. Down at the end of the pier. She appeared to be alone, but from the way she was shaking and staring off to her left, I knew that she wasn't. Without thinking, I took off down the pier running as fast I could. The pier seemed to be growing, getting longer and longer with each stride I took. She was now even farther away than when I started. Suddenly, a figure came out from the shadows, grabbed her around the waist, and pushed her toward the water. I froze. I just stood there and watched as she was thrown into the freezing lake.

***

I woke up in a cold sweat, screaming. It took me a moment to remember where I was. Last night, after chasing Allison's scent around in circles for hours, I was too exhausted to go home and face my father. So I went back to the Wright's house. Someone must have known that I would be coming here, or maybe they left the door open in case Allison came home on her own. Either way, I was relieved to find the door unlocked and was able to get out of the cold. I probably should have slept on the couch in the family room, but I didn't. I don't even remember walking up the stairs, or opening the door to her room, but I woke up in her bed, wrapped in her scent.

"Hey man, you okay? I heard you screaming," Aiden said as he busted into Alli's room.

I felt embarrassed, being caught in Alli's bed, even though she was not here with me. It still felt awkward. The situation became even more humiliating when Mr. Wright came in with a cold rag in one hand, and without a second thought, said, "Good morning guys."

"Good morning, Mr. Wright," I said getting out of Alli's bed.

Mr. Wright put his hand on my shoulder and told me that it was okay and that I should stay put. Then he put his hand on my forehead, which made the situation stranger. I had seen mothers and fathers do this to their children to see if they had a temperature, but being a werewolf, no one had ever done that to me.

"I heard you come in last night. Man, you are still burning up. Here, take these," he said.

"It's okay, Mr. Wright. I don't feel that bad, plus I don't think they will work on me," I said waving off the small white pills.

"That's what Lillian said, but it's just some aspirin. I don't see how it can hurt. You never know until you try."

I took the aspirin and walked to Allison's bathroom to get a cup of water. I was willing to try anything to feel better. And judging from the look of my reflection in the mirror, I needed to. By the time I came out of the bathroom, both Aiden and Mr. Wright had left.

***

It may have been kind of odd, but it was also comforting being at the Wright's house this morning, and honestly, I think the aspirin might have helped a little. I was feeling better, if only slightly, by the time my search party met up. The plan was to search the opposite side of the lake today, which included the Wright house. So, we all decided that we might as well start right there.

Searching through Alli's stuff was just too much for me. It was difficult seeing people touching her personal belongings, even though they were my pack mates, and I've known them all my life. I found the note that I slipped into her locker asking her to meet me, in her nightstand, and it made my heart throb. It was then that I decided to take a break and get some fresh air.

I was sitting on the porch talking to Aiden about what's next in the search when Gage pulled up in his car.

"Hey man, how are you holding up?" Gage asked as he walked over to me and shook my hand.

"I'm hanging in there, man. Hey, have you met Alli's brother, Aiden?" I asked.

Aiden walked over and shook Gage's hand, "Oh yeah, we've met. What's going on?"

Gage pointed to his car and said, "Gotta get my car searched. I wasn't home yesterday when you guys came by, so I thought I would bring the car to you.

It sure would be nice if everyone on the estate was as understanding and accommodating as Gage. I would bet my life that Kendall's not going to come driving up so that we could take a look in her car. I guess I still looked a bit worn out because Aiden stepped up and said, "I got this one."

I walked down to the end of the driveway and stood there just staring out into the woods thinking about Alli. I hoped that she was at least somewhere inside. She hated the cold and it has been getting colder and colder as we got closer to Thanksgiving. And with the way the wind was picking up, it looked like a winter storm was on the way.

A strong blast of wind blew in from the north and what it carried with it caused chills to come up on my arms and my nose to twitch. I smelled Alli and her scent was strong. I followed my nose to the source of the smell. I was shocked to find that it was the trunk of Gage's car.

Stunned, I stared down into the trunk. It looked just like all the other trunks that we searched with one exception, my damn alpha ring. My ears started ringing, my pulse quickened, and my vision tunneled. I wanted Gage's head on a stick, and I wanted to be the one to rip it off. Immediately, people were on me trying to hold me back. Gage looked terrified, and he sure the fuck should have been.

It took both of Allison's parents to calm me down enough to find out what Gage knew. Gage told us that he had let his friend, Dylan, borrow his car. Dylan, the asshole who was following Alli in the woods. The one whom I warned to leave my estate and never look back. It was time to find that bastard... and kill him.

Chapter 55

Allison

My senses came back to me slowly, and it took me a minute to remember where I was. With my brain still in a bit of a fog, I cracked my eyes open just wide enough to see who was with me, scared that Kendall might inject me again with whatever the hell she used to knock me out the first time. Who knew for how long I was out. It could have been the next day; it could have been three days as far as I could tell.

I saw Dylan sitting in the living room watching television, and he appeared to be alone, so I sat up and looked around, hoping to spot the vile Kendall used to drug me. My movement caught Dylan's attention, and within no time, he was at my side staring down at me with a wicked grin.

"Slept well?"

"What the hell did she inject me with? That's so not cool," I said as I rubbed the tender spot on my neck where the needle had gone in.

"Yeah, to be honest, it kind of shocked me too. She doesn't mess around, does she? Don't worry though. It's nothing that will hurt you. Her uncle keeps the shit around in case they need to tranquilize any unruly werewolves. That's what she said, anyway."

He looked around as if to make sure no one else was listening, leaned in, and confided, "Kind of makes you wonder what really goes on at this place, huh?"

Unsure of how to respond, I just sat there staring at him in disbelief. My entire body ached, and more than anything, I wanted to get out of the bed, but that wasn't going to be an option being that I was tied to it. Without any other option, I lay back and tried to get comfortable, but as soon as my head hit the pillow, it began to throb too. I clinched my eyes shut and reached up to massage my temples.

Little beads of sweat started forming on my forehead, and I knew that I must have a fever.

Dylan came over, put his hand on my head, and asked, "Hey, are you alright? You look like hell."

The sound of his voice made my head pound even worse, and suddenly, it was painful just to speak. "My head hurts. Can I get some water or something? Is there anything to eat in this place?"

He backed up, staring at me in deep thought, then finally spoke, "Yeah, sure. Let me go take a look around."

I knew he was most likely contemplating whether or not my sudden illness was from the drugs or from being apart from Cade. Surely, he was wondering how much longer they had to keep me around. The longer they kept me here, the riskier their little plan became.

Hearing Dylan banging around in the kitchen, I closed my eyes and concentrated on breathing slowly and deeply in and out. Shooting pains, throbbing pains, stabbing pains, you name it, they were present, and seemed to be spreading. Without warning, my stomach clinched, and it felt like a knot the size of Texas was invading my body. If I wasn't tied up like a chick in a bad skin-flick, I'd curl up in a ball and pray for the pain to stop.

Dylan called out from the kitchen, "I'm getting you some water, but there ain't shit to eat here. Looks like I'll have to put a call into the boss-lady. Maybe she will grab us some grub on her way back over."

Boss-lady? Since when had Kendall become in charge. Here I thought Dylan was the mastermind in this whole scheme. Hearing that one little comment, it became clear what I needed to do. I needed to push the pain aside and take advantage of my time here alone with Dylan. If I was going to get out of here, it would definitely be through him. Kendall wasn't going to let me go; I'm guessing my release or escape would be over her dead body.

After a few more deep breaths, I asked, "Hey Dylan, can you come in here for a minute?" Now sweating profusely, I knew I must look like utter shit, so while I probably couldn't count on my seductive nature to win him over, I was hoping my power of persuasion might work. And I was kind of hoping his need for power was stronger than his lust for Kendall.

Giving him a sheepish grin, I asked, "Can you move my hair out of my face, please." He swept my hair back behind my ears. My throbbing head was making this more difficult, and my acting skills have never been first-rate, but if I was going to get out of here, I needed to try something.

He backed up a bit and said, "There. Is that better?"

"Yeah, thanks."

"You are really sweating. I think you may have a fever. Here drink some water."

I gulped down the cold water, and it relieved the tightness in my stomach a bit but that only gave way to the nausea. Feeling as if I may puke any second wasn't helping, but I needed to try something... anything, before Kendall returned.

"So Dylan, why do you need Kendall anyway? I mean, have you really thought this through? She really is an obnoxious bitch. Do you really want to be her mate when all of this is said and done? You know, when you're alpha, do you really want her by your side? Can you imagine her as a wife? Can you imagine her raising your children?"

He looked at me, clearly shocked by the words coming out of my mouth. When he didn't respond, I continued, "I just can't figure out why you are letting her run the show. Why you even need her, really. Once you are alpha, don't you want to pick your mate? Someone who you really want to be with? Someone more like... oh, I don't know. Someone like me."

Dylan rolled his eyes at me and then turned away. I hoped that he was thinking about it, but I had a feeling that he was going to stick with her.

With his back to me, he said, "I don't need to explain things to you. I have my reasons for needing Kendall, so you can stop trying to get me to turn on her. It isn't going to work."

Though I couldn't see his face, the tone of his voice told me I had hit a nerve. "Just sayin'. I hope you've thought your little plan through. This could end quite badly, you know."

Dylan walked out of the room, but before he left, he said, "I'll call Kendall and see if we can get you some food."

With Dylan gone, I laid back and stared at the ceiling. I definitely had a fever, needed badly to throw up, and my head felt like it had a jackhammer in it. Things were looking pretty hopeless, especially if I was only going to get worse being away from Cade. My only hope was that he finds me, and soon.

Chapter 56

Kendall

The next morning when I woke up, I needed to get away from my house, away from my mother, away from anything that would remind me of how badly I have screwed everything up. It would be a miracle if Dylan and I got away with our plan, which was becoming more and more screwed up by the minute. One wrong step could send our whole scheme crashing down, and until the search parties stop their investigation of the estate, I won't be able to breathe.

I could only begin to imagine what my mother would do if Dylan and I were caught, and I damaged her status in the pack further. She wouldn't care less what would become of me, just like she all but forgot about my father when he was sent away for his "misconduct." She rarely spoke of him, hardly a word since he left. And only then, it was to remind me of how horribly he screwed up our lives.

I snuck out of the house, knowing Mom would be sleeping off a hangover, and went straight to Shari's. Surely, she'd have some questions, I had yet to face her since I busted out of the pack meeting, but I didn't know where else to go. I considered heading over to check on Dylan, but I figured it was best to stay away from there as much as possible. I had to trust that Dylan was taking care of things.

As I pulled into Shari's driveway, I grabbed my phone out of my purse to check for any texts. Nothing new. With my phone in hand, I headed up to the door, but before I could knock, Shari swung open the front door and pulled me inside.

"Thank God you're here. What is going on? You stormed out of the meeting like a bat out of hell, and I was waiting for you to call. I thought you might need some time to digest everything, but I was just about to go find you," Shari exclaimed as she pulled me by the arm all the way over to the couch in her living room.

I sat down, placing my purse and phone on the coffee table. It was time to be honest… well sort of honest, anyway. "What is going on is that I'm totally screwed. If Cade and Allison are really true mates, then that means that we are really finished. For good. It's over Shari. Really over." Just hearing those words made my eyes water, but I refused to cry, even if it was the first time that I admitted out loud that Cade and I were over. Things were never going to be the same, and if things worked out the way they were supposed to, Cade would be dead soon and the real work would begin.

Did I really want Cade dead? It was the first time I really thought about it. Could I actually go through with this?

Shari's words interrupted my thoughts. "I'm so sorry Kendall. Have you seen him? Cade, I mean. Did he say anything to you?"

I looked away, trying to hide the fact that what I wanted more than anything was to just sit there and cry. Cry because I had really lost Cade, cry because deep in my heart, I knew that I should have never gotten involved with Dylan, cry because nothing would ever be the same again no matter how this whole thing turned out.

What is wrong with me? I need to get it together. I can do this! I have to do this. There isn't any other option now. Dylan and I have to get rid of Allison and Cade. No excuses! It is too damn late to turn back now.

Without looking back in her direction, I admitted, "No… I haven't talked to him, but I knew something was going on. I just didn't want to say anything. You understand, don't you?"

When I turned back, she was smiling reassuringly. "Sure, I get it. This really sucks, huh?"

Shari couldn't have said it better. "Yes, it really does," I whined. And with that, Shari threw her arm over my shoulder, giving me a little squeeze. "Well, I know what makes me feel better when everything else around me seems completely sucky. How about we get out of here, go eat an enormously fattening breakfast, and shop the day away?"

Just then, footsteps pounded their way down the stairs. Within seconds, Shari's mom found us in the living room and frantically exclaimed, "You won't believe it! The search is off. Cade's alpha ring was found in the truck of Gage's car! But it wasn't Gage. Noel told me that it was someone named Dylan. Apparently, this guy borrowed

Gage's car a few nights ago. The same night that Allison went missing! They are pretty sure they are on the right track. Now they just need to find him, which shouldn't be too hard for a pack of werewolves."

As soon as Shari's mom paused to take a breath, Shari said, "Oh my God, Mom! Do they have any idea where this Dylan guy could be? They've got to find him fast before he does something to Allison."

Now, Shari was in a panic. I needed to channel my inner actress and fast! I jumped up from the couch and shouted, "I can't believe they finally have a lead. That is great news! Are they searching for him now?"

"Yes, both search parties are teaming up right now to make a plan of attack and decide whether or not to alert the authorities at this point. So, it won't be long before they begin their hunt."

Not good! I had to get the hell out of there and get to Dylan immediately. Before anything else was said, I looked down at my watch, grabbed my purse, and hurried toward the door. "Sorry guys but I got to go. I completely forgot that I had plans with my mom. I need to tell her the news. She might want to help. Shari, call me later, okay? Especially if there is any new info about the search." I closed the door behind me before they could respond and ran out to my car. I needed to get to Dylan before someone else did.

Chapter 57

Cade

I didn't know what the elders were thinking. How did they expect me to sit here and be civil? They knew that it went against everything that I was feeling, everything that was natural. My mate had been kidnapped by a guest on our estate, and my body was twitching and begging me to let my instincts take over and hunt the bastard down. I was doing my best to stay in control, but I was not sure how much longer I could wait.

After realizing that it was Dylan Christianson that we were looking for, the elders called for an immediate pack meeting at the Lodge to plan our next move. Half of the pack wanted to involve the local authorities and turn the search over to them. The other half felt that since Dylan was a were, we should handle this ordeal ourselves. Personally, I wanted to take care of him all by myself, but I knew that the elders would never let that happen.

There were so many conversations going on at the same time, it made it hard to listen in on any one in particular, so I didn't mind when Shari came over and sat down next to me.

"Hey, Cade, how are you holding up?" Shari asked tapping me on the knee.

Trying my best to smile, I said, "I'm hanging in there, thanks for asking. I know things are pretty weird around here."

"You can say that again. So, is Allison your true mate, really?"

"Yeah, she is," I told her as I looked down at my hands.

"Wow, I didn't know that still happened. I mean, it's been a really long time since someone around here actually *mated*. That must be awesome, you know, for you and Alli."

I hate awkward silences. Apparently, so did Shari.

"Hey, is Kendall here? Have you seen her?" she asked.

"I don't think that she's here." I paused. "Shari, I swear I never meant to hurt Kendall. You know I would never do that, right?" I asked hoping that she would understand.

"I know you didn't. I just feel so bad for her, you know? She's been so frazzled lately. She even left my house today in such a rush that she forgot her phone. Kendall never goes anywhere without her phone," Shari said holding out Kendall's pink jeweled phone.

When I didn't say anything more, Shari got up and went to sit with her family. The meeting finally began with a lengthy discussion about our options. We didn't know where Dylan was or even where to start looking, but the few who knew him, offered some suggestions. We did know that he probably wasn't too far since he was seen on the estate just a few days ago, and most of the elders agreed that there had to be some reason that he abducted Allison, so it was likely he would stay nearby.

Again the pack was split up into search parties, and again my father tried to keep me here. My involvement in the search sparked yet another heated debate among the pack. I sat there quietly, the rage building inside me.

I can't believe for one second that anyone in this room doesn't realize that I'm going, whether they agree or not. Allison is my mate. If anyone is going to go searching for her, I am. Sick or not!

"That's enough!" yelled Mrs. Wright. "We are wasting valuable time here. My daughter has been kidnapped and gone for days. I don't care how we do this, but I want her found."

Finally, the arguing ended and the room became quiet... quiet until Kendall's phone began to ring. I looked over at Shari, who was frantically trying to silence the stupid phone. You could tell she was completely humiliated and from the look on her mom's face, words would be exchanged after the meeting. Cell phones were off limits in the Lodge.

The next time I glanced at Shari, she was up and heading in my direction.

"Cade, I need to talk to you outside," she whispered.

"Can't it wait, Shari?" I asked.

"No, I don't think it can," she said with a worried expression on her face. She got up and headed to the back exit.

I tapped Aiden on the shoulder and told him where I was going. He asked if he could come with me, claiming that he needed some fresh air, but I suspected that Mrs. Wright had asked him to keep an eye on me. She has been checking on me every few hours. All I could figure was that she hoped that as long as I was okay that Alli would be too. Little did she know I was doing my very best to put on a brave face; otherwise, I knew the elders, mainly my father, wouldn't allow me to participate in the search. The truth was my entire body felt like my insides were attacking each other. It was like the Civil War was taking place inside me.

At first I didn't see Shari outside, but then she came out from behind the supply shed and scared the piss out of me.

"Jesus Shari. What's with the black ops shit? I nearly had a heart attack," Aiden said grabbing his chest.

"I'm sorry. I just don't want anyone to see us. What if I'm wrong? I don't know... it's probably nothing, but... just look," Shari said handing me Kendall's cell phone.

Bring snacks to the cabin our little friend is hungry

I read the text twice, not wanting to think what I was thinking. Kendall couldn't be involved in this. Could she? I knew that she was pissed and she probably hated me now, but she was not an evil person. Was she?

Aiden took the phone from me and read the text out loud.

"Do you two think this is about Al?" Aiden asked.

When nobody answered him, he said, "Okay, well, where is this cabin?"

That's when it clicked. Kendall's mom had a ski cabin just outside of the estate. We used to sneak out there when we were younger. It was only about fifteen minutes from where we were standing. I took Kendall's phone from Aiden and put it in my pocket. My body was failing me and my mind seemed to be having a panic attack.

Where is my car? Will I get there faster on all fours? Does Kendall realize what she has done?

"Maybe, Kendall's ski cabin?!" Shari yelled a little late.

"Shari is your car here?" I asked.

"Yeah, I'm parked on the corner. Why?"

"Give me your keys."

Shari handed me the keys, and I took off running. It wasn't until I was putting the car in drive that I realized that Aiden was riding shotgun.

Chapter 58

Allison

Dylan hasn't said two words to me since I unsuccessfully tried to convince him to turn against Kendall. Though I knew my little plan had a very low chance of working, I couldn't help but be bummed. And freaked-out. And terrified. And... well, I could go on and on. It was time to face the facts, and the facts were telling me that things weren't likely to go my way. And as long as I'm being honest with myself, as each minute passed, I was becoming more and more discouraged. A magic eight ball would surely be saying "outlook not so good" right at this very moment.

Dylan left me alone in the bedroom, still tied to the bed, while he watched television in the living room. At least, he left my television on the TLC channel. There was always something on worthy of passing the time. Before he left the room, he did promise that I will have some food soon, which was good, since I had a feeling that my insides were beginning to eat themselves. Starving just didn't seem like a strong enough word for it; though it wasn't just my stomach that hurt. Everything hurt, and I had a feeling that it wasn't just because I was hungry.

I knew I was growing weaker by the minute. I must try to change again. One last Hail Mary! I gathered up every last ounce of strength I had left for this last attempt, and... nearly passed out. Yeah, this was not going to work.

Mid-way though the third episode of *A Baby Story*, Kendall busted through the door in a frenzy. I heard her throwing stuff around as she shouted, "Get your ass off the couch, Dylan. We have to get out of here now. They know it was you, and unless you want an entire pack of angry wolves after you, we need to move!"

Dylan, now equally as panicked as Kendall, jumped up and was moving immediately. Stuffing his belongings in a duffle-bag, he chastised, "Well, why the hell didn't you text me? I could have been long-gone already!"

"Don't you think I would have if I had my phone? I think I left it at Shari's when I high-tailed it out of there as soon as her mom told us that the search parties' new target was you. Apparently, we didn't search the trunk as well as we thought before you gave the car back to Gage because Cade's alpha ring was in it. How the hell did we miss that? That asshole must have given Alli his ring. I can't believe this! At least, they have no idea where we are."

I couldn't see much of what was going on in the other room, but for a brief moment, there was silence, as if suddenly they both stopped moving, and finally, Dylan asked, "You did get my text about the food, right? Before you left your phone. Tell me you got my text about the food!"

The commotion instantly resumed as Kendall screamed, "NO! I didn't see it! Please tell me you didn't mention Allison or the cabin. Oh shit! Dylan, this is really bad."

Dylan and Kendall flew through the bedroom door and began packing up around me, though neither acknowledged my existence as they shoved things into their bags. Dylan stopped moving and said, "I may have mentioned something about the cabin."

Kendall dropped the shirt that was in her hand and answered, "Then we need to move now. Grab the girl, and I'll get the bags. But keep her hands and feet tied. We don't need any more trouble."

Dylan tossed me over his shoulder like a sack of potatoes and said, "Looks like we are taking a drive. Your little boyfriend may be on to us. But don't worry. There is no way in hell that I'm giving up. We are in way too deep to give up now. Your best bet is just to sit back and behave yourself so you don't get hurt."

Before I knew it, I was half-sitting, half-laying across the back seat of Kendall's car, Dylan was in the driver's seat, and Kendall was shouting at him to get moving. Dylan slammed on the gas, and we were heading down the path that lead back out to the main road.

As Kendall and Dylan shouted orders back and forth between the two of them, I did my best to straighten my body so that I was at least sitting and could see what was going on in front of me. Though my wrists and ankles were still tied, my hands were fastened in front of me, making it much easier to find a position that wasn't too painful.

Dylan made it to the end of the path and took a quick right out on to the main road leading away from the estate. Kendall threw her head around to look out the back windshield and terror filled her eyes. "You are going to have to move faster than that! They are behind us!"

Dylan adjusted the rearview mirror and floored the gas pedal. "Holy shit, Kendall. How did they get here so quick? What the hell are we going to do?"

"Just drive, you idiot. And try to lose them!"

I twisted around just in time to catch a glimpse of Cade and Aiden in the car behind us. They weren't too far behind, and they appeared to be speeding up, which hopefully meant that they knew that it was us in the car in front of them.

With Kendall and Dylan screaming at each other, I turned back around to look out the back window and did my best to signal to Cade that I was in the car. His eyes met mine and immediately that familiar itchy feeling rushed throughout my body, and I knew it wouldn't be long before I found myself on all fours. There was no way that I could stop the change, not once it started. That I hadn't quite mastered yet. I needed to make my move, and it was now or never.

Without a second thought, I threw my tied arms over Dylan's head and pulled as hard as I could, hoping to strangle him or at the very least distract him. Before Kendall could react, Dylan swerved off the road and our car was tumbling into a ditch.

The car came to a halt upside down. Kendall, who was thrown from the car, lay only a few feet away, bleeding, and struggling to get up. I no longer needed to worry about the ropes that were once restraining my human arms and legs, I had shifted.

Hackles spiked, I slinked out of the car's broken window, gave a low, deep growl, and lunged at Kendall's throat.

Chapter 59

Cade

"No!" I screamed. It all happened in slow motion, just like in the movies. Though I couldn't be exactly sure as to what had happened in the car in front of me, it appeared that Allison threw her arms over Dylan's head from the backseat. Only a moment later, I watched as Kendall's car swerved off the road, flipped over, and landed in the shallow ditch below.

"Pull over, pull over!" Aiden shouted from the passenger seat, but I barely heard him over my own thoughts. *Alli has to be okay. She has to. Oh my God! How can this be happening!*

My mind racing, I managed to pull the car over and rush toward the smashed up, overturned vehicle, but stopped dead in my tracks when I saw two wolves emerge from the backside of the wreckage.

Relief washed over me when I saw that one of the two wolves was Allison. She was alive and safe. The other was Dylan. There he was, only a few hundred feet in front of me. Our eyes connected, and he turned and started running the opposite direction. I couldn't believe that after everything he did, the coward was trying to run away from me.

Not going to happen.

The mere thought of him getting away triggered my immediate transformation, and while I was only vaguely aware of what was going on around me, I knew that Kendall was now up, but it was only for a second before Allison sprung toward her like a blood-thirsty beast. I had to force myself to remain focused on getting to Dylan.

Running after Dylan, like a wolf possessed, I prayed that Allison would be okay. There was just no way that I could let Dylan get away with this. Surely, Aiden could help Allison take Kendall down, but before I took off, Aiden was, for some reason, still human. Could

Allison hold her own long enough for me to take down Dylan? I hoped so because I ran. Ran after the first wolf, who would most certainly die at my hands because after I chase him down, I had every intention of ripping his head off.

The chase was over within a few minutes. With speed and pure rage on my side, I bit into his hind leg before he even had the chance to check behind him to gauge my distance. Dylan was strong, but I was stronger, even in my weakened state. With an injured ankle, Dylan rolled to the ground, and within no time, I was on top of him.

We traded blow for blow a few times, before I decided to stop playing with my food. I didn't have time to mess around, not when Allison could be in danger. I sank my teeth into the soft, fleshy area under his shoulder. He yelped, but somehow managed to make it to his feet, and limped back a few feet.

He stumbled back, trying to regain his footing, when he spotted Aiden running toward us. Aiden froze when Dylan bared his teeth at him. Though seriously wounded, Dylan took off toward Aiden and wasted no time attacking him. Aiden in human form was no match for a werewolf, even an injured one.

Why had I even let the bastard get to his feet? This was my fault. I should have finished Dylan off when I had the chance, but I hesitated, and now Aiden was paying for it.

I wasn't going to reach them in time. In one quick movement, Dylan had tossed Aiden up into the air like a rag doll and slammed him face first into a tree. Aiden was laying there on the ground, unconscious and bleeding from his head when I dashed to his side. I lunged for Dylan, but not before he grabbed Aiden again and ripped open his shoulder, the tear was so deep that I could see the muscle hanging loosely from the bone.

Just before Dylan could finish him off, I jumped toward him and knocked him down. I had him pinned to the ground and closed my teeth around his neck. Thrashing my head from side to side, I heard his neck pop. It may have been my first kill, but I knew Dylan was dead. The look of death in his eyes was unmistakable.

There was no time to think about what I had done. Allison needed me. I rushed over to where Allison and Kendall were still fighting, and was shocked to see that Alli was actually holding her own. Kendall was always a good, strong fighter, but, apparently, so was Allison. When I reached them, Alli was on top, but Kendall thrashed until she managed to get back to her feet. Kendall gave a deep growl and prepared to pounce.

Rushing Kendall from behind, I latched on to her hind leg, pulled her back with my teeth, and pinned her down under my weight. I prepared myself for what I might have to do to her. I expected a struggle. I expected her to fight me with everything she had after all that had occurred, but she didn't. Her eyes met mine, and she just gave up. I guess she wasn't as strong as I thought she was, or maybe she just knew that it was over. She couldn't win this time.

"Omigod, Cade! Is that Aiden?" Alli screamed her voice full of worry.

I turned abruptly, to find Alli, now human, rushing to her brother's side. The sight of Aiden's mangled body must have triggered her change. After that, my transformation was immediate, and I hurried to the trunk of Shari's car and found a blanket, a towel, and her spare set of sweats for Alli.

I handed Alli the clothes and the towel and said, "Put these on and use the towel to hold pressure to Aiden's wounds. Try to staunch the blood. He is losing too much." Wrapping the blanket around my waist, I went to grab my phone to call the Lodge for help. As soon as they were on the way, I grabbed Kendall's clothes from the back of her wrecked car and tossed them to her.

"Here, Kendall. Get dressed. My dad should be here any minute, so don't even think about moving," I warned.

Kendall said something under her breath as she reached for the clothes, but it was a comment not meant for me, and it didn't matter anyway. She knew better than to try to get away, and she should be thankful that I gave her something to wear. Kendall was wrong, and I will never forgive her for what she did to me and to Alli, but it's not right to humiliate her by leaving her naked when everyone arrives, even if she does deserve it.

"Help is on the way," I said as I leaned down to help Aiden. I took over applying pressure to his wound, giving Alli the opportunity to comfort her brother. When I heard the first siren, the words *thank God* escaped from my lips. The bleeding from Aiden's shoulder wound didn't seem to be slowing, and even being a were, I wasn't sure how much longer he would last if help didn't arrive soon. There was nothing else we could do for him; he needed a doctor… fast.

When the estate's ambulance arrived, along with half the pack, it was complete chaos. People yelling and arguing. People running around and barking orders. People crying and praying. The whole time, I never let go of Allison's hand. I couldn't. Even when her parents hurried over to hug her, I couldn't let go.

When things finally calmed down a bit, I was able to take my first real look at her.

"Are you hurt? Let me see your face," I told her pulling her up to me and gently wiping a speck of blood from her cheek. She looked tired, and bruised, but absolutely beautiful. The only thing that mattered was that she was safe, and I would do anything to make sure she stayed that way.

Chapter 60

Kendall

Sitting on the side of the road, I felt the first real tears I've cried in a long time roll down my face. My fate now lied in someone else's hands, and there was nothing I could do about it. It felt like I was waiting on death row. Werewolf law didn't work like human law. I had planned to kill the alpha's son, and Marcus may very well kill me for it.

I sat waiting, watching Allison and Cade try to save Aiden. He looked dead already. Lifeless. Ripped to shreds, but they loved him, cared about him. They would do whatever it took to save him.

And then there was me. Dylan was dead, and I didn't even have it in me to care. *What kind of person am I?* He was supposed to be my mate one day, and all I could think about was the fact that now I was left to face the consequences of both of our actions.

When the ambulance arrived, our resident EMS and doctor hurried out to access the situation. Only moments later, several other members of the pack arrived, including Marcus. He didn't even look my way until Aiden was loaded into the ambulance, and Allison, her family, and Cade were instructed to head to the pack's infirmary. Apparently, a blood transfusion would be in order, but the doctor seemed hopeful that Aiden will survive. No human could have made it, but lucky for him, weres heal rapidly.

With everyone else being sent on their way, there was only me left to be dealt with. Marcus turned my way and demanded, "Kendall, get in the car."

There was no way that I was going to disobey. In this situation, I wasn't even at liberty to speak, so I ducked my head and headed to the backseat of his vehicle. Not a word was spoken on the way back, and in the silence, I tried desperately to come up with an excuse for my behavior. Any excuse, even a bad one, would be better than admitting my plan to take over the pack with Dylan.

With Dylan gone, it didn't matter what I said. He was dead. What harm would there be in throwing him under the bus? But would Marcus believe me? I could say I was forced. That Dylan threatened to kill me if I didn't help him. That he threatened to kill my mom too. But in my heart, I knew that it didn't matter what I said. Marcus would never believe me, and even if he did, he would say that I should have come to him for help. That he could have saved me.

Pulling into the alpha's driveway, my heart rate increased, and I could feel my eyes beginning to water once again. With my emotions on overdrive, I stepped out of his car and followed him up his front steps. Before he could get his key in the lock, Noel opened the door and stepped back to allow us in. My mother, who was on the couch, immediately stood as she saw us enter. Still, no words were spoken. I was led over to my mom, and to my surprise, the frigid bitch pulled me in for a hug. But in my ear, she whispered, "You really fucked us over this time."

Marcus stood in front of us all and finally spoke. "Have a seat, ladies."

We all sat, Noel included, and I attempted to mentally prepare myself for what was to come.

Marcus didn't waste any time getting down to business. He poured himself a glass of water from the pitcher that had been sat out on the coffee table, took a small sip, and began, "Well, there isn't much to say. I'm not interested in hearing your excuses, Kendall. What you did is inexcusable, and therefore, you and your mother will hereby be exiled from the estate. You are to pack your things and leave tonight."

My mother's hand flew over her mouth but not before a loud gasp escaped. "Marcus, please no! Just hear Kendall out. I'm sure you will rethink your decision," Mother pleaded.

"I'm sorry, but my decision is final. Your daughter kidnapped a member of our pack, my son's mate, for God's sake. And I can only imagine what else those two had planned. You can't think for a moment, that I believe they were just going to let Allison go. This was all in attempt to hurt Cade, or worse. I'm no fool, Claire; please don't play me for one."

My mom glanced my way, and then lowered her voice an octave as if I could no longer hear her if she spoke a bit more quietly. "But why me, Marcus? This was Kendall's doing, not mine. Why am I to be punished for her wrong-doings?"

Was my own mother actually asking him to banish me and not her? What? Just send me off into the world to fend for myself? I knew she was a pathetic excuse for a mother, but this was unbelievable.

When Marcus looked my way, I could have sworn there was sympathy in his eyes. Even he knew how horrid my mother was.

Noel spoke up, surprising us all. "Marcus, may I speak freely?"

He placed his hand on his wife's and said, "Of course, dear."

Her attention was directed solely on my mother as she said, "Claire, frankly I'm appalled that you would be willing to send Kendall away by herself. You really never knew how to be a mother, did you? Well, I can tell you why you are leaving here tonight with your daughter. There is only one person to blame for Kendall's behavior. And it's you. You are the reason your daughter has become a cold-hearted bitch. You're the reason that she very well could have become a murderer had her and Dylan not have been stopped. You, Claire. Don't think for one moment that Marcus and I don't realize that. You have never cared about anyone but yourself and your status in this pack. You pressured Kendall to help raise your family's rank, and the only reason we didn't stop you was because Cade seemed to genuinely love Kendall, and we wanted Cade's happiness above anything else. That's what real parents do. They love their children more than they love themselves, more than anything else. You will leave here tonight, and there is nothing you can say or do to change our minds."

After that, my mother was speechless. And it kind of felt good to know that Marcus and Noel knew the score. That they didn't blame me completely.

Marcus stood, wordlessly telling us that this meeting was adjourned, but before we left, he said one last thing. "And just so you know, Kendall. You are lucky that you are still breathing. I should kill you. And if it were anyone else, I probably would. You plotted against my son, and almost killed his mate. Don't think for one second, that if you ever return, for any reason, that I won't kill you, because you would be wrong. You have two hours to evacuate the premises. Take only what belongs to you. I have arranged for a cab to pick you up and take you wherever you choose to go. Now leave, and I suggest that you don't look back."

My mother and I walked out the door together, but there had never been more distance between us than there was at that moment. There was no telling what my future held, but I had a good feeling that she wouldn't be a part of it.

Chapter 61

Cade

I freakin' hate hospitals. I hate the antiseptic smell and the bright fluorescent lights. I hate the way everyone just stands around waiting for the news that either their loved ones will be okay or they won't. Even in our little infirmary on the estate, it felt the same. All of the excitement of the evening had long ago faded, and the only people left here were members of the Wright family and me. The elders had all gone home, with the exception of Alli's grandparents, but I couldn't leave, even though I probably should.

With Aiden in a serious condition, I felt like this was way too personal for an outsider to witness. But I just couldn't leave Alli. Not yet.

So many things about tonight were confusing the hell out of me. *Why did Dylan choose this pack to torment? When did Kendall become such an unfeeling bitch? Why didn't Aiden transform when he was attacked?* I should just stop thinking about questions that I will more than likely never know the answers to.

"Okay everyone, I'm going to need you out for a while," the doctor said.

Alli and I walked out of Aiden's small room and into the quiet waiting room down the hall. I pulled her close to me so that I could rest my chin on the top of her head. We just stood there, holding each other until the doctor came in.

"Mr. and Mrs. Wright, I'm afraid that my initial thought was correct. Aiden has lost too much blood, he's going to need a transfusion," the doctor confirmed.

Beside me, I heard Alli gasp. I gave her a reassuring squeeze, but on the inside, I knew that this was bad. I have never heard of a werewolf needing a blood transfusion, but hell, before I met Alli, I have never heard of a werewolf getting sick either.

"Which one of you is B positive?" I heard the doctor ask. Mr. and Mrs. Wright looked at each other and then asked to speak to the doctor in private.

As they walked to the end of the hall to talk, I all but collapsed on the small leather sofa. I hadn't realized just how exhausted I was until now. I was already feeling a thousand times better just being with Alli, but still not 100 percent.

It's weird the way this mating thing worked. One minute, I felt like I was on my death bed, but then was strong enough to defeat a rogue the next, and all it took was one look at Alli.

"How are you holding up?" Alli asked, sitting down beside me.

"I'm fine… I'm good. Just tired and worried," I told her.

"Baby, why don't you go home, take a hot shower, and get some rest. I promise I'll call you as soon as there is some news," Alli assured me.

I reached over and pulled her onto my lap. I couldn't stand to be separated from her, not even for a short while. I gently rubbed her back and whispered in her ear, "Don't. Please. I can't. I need to be with you. Just let me stay with you, okay?" She didn't say anything; she didn't need to. She just took my face between her hands and kissed me. It was a quick, soft, little kiss, but it was just what I needed. That kiss meant the beginning of our new lives together.

I was leaning in to steal another kiss, when Mr. and Mrs. Wright came into the room. They both looked worried and nervous, which was to be expected after all that had occurred. I didn't know how they kept their spirits up, but they did. They sat down opposite of us in the waiting room.

"Cade, your father is on the way up here," Mr. Wright said.

Strangely, I was actually relieved that he was coming here. There was a nagging at the back of my mind since I watched the life drain out of Dylan's eyes, and I knew that only my father would understand what I was feeling. I did what I had to do. I knew that, but that didn't stop me from feeling sick about it. I didn't want to bother Alli with it though. She had enough to worry about with her brother. She didn't need to hear how guilty I felt about killing the wolf who had kidnapped her, and very nearly killed her brother.

"We need to talk to both of you before Marcus arrives," Mrs. Wright said looking down at her shaky hands.

"What is it, Mom? Is Aiden going to be okay?" Alli asked in a panic.

"He will, as soon as Marcus gets here."

"What does my father have to do with Aiden's recovery?" I asked.

"Oh God, how can I say this?" Mrs. Wright asked with tears forming in her eyes.

"Aiden needs his blood. Cade, your father, is also Aiden's father," Mr. Wright said, so that his wife wouldn't have to.

I felt Alli stiffen in my arms as my own breath caught in my throat. My mind started racing, trying to process what I just heard. *My father is Aiden's father. That would make us half-brothers. A brother? Wait, does that mean I'm related to Alli? Think damn-it... no? Thank God. That would be bad.*

"I have a brother," I whispered to myself, kind of liking the way it sounded. As an only child, I have always wanted a brother.

Alli turned and stared right in my eyes, "No, he is my brother."

I was slightly taken aback by her remark, but I tried to imagine how she must have felt. This was all too much for us to handle.

"Cade is right, and so are you, honey. The truth is that I was pregnant with Marcus's child when I fled from the estate all those years ago. I didn't know until I had already left. And to be honest, I wasn't sure that I would be welcomed back. And I really didn't want to go back. So I stayed... I started a new life with your father," Mrs. Wright told Alli.

"But I don't understand. Dad, did you just find out? Oh God, Dad, that is so awful. I'm so sorry—," Alli was saying until she was cut off.

"No, baby. I knew from the beginning. Why don't you just take some time to let this all sink in, and I promise we can talk about this later, when Aiden can be here to listen," Mr. Wright said.

Without another word, Mr. and Mrs. Wright got up and went back into Aiden's room.

Alli tried to scoot off from my lap, but I just held her tighter. We would figure this out, we had to.

"I'm sorry. I didn't mean to snap at you," Alli whispered.

I placed a kiss on her nose and said, "He was going to be my brother one day anyway."

Just then, my parents came busting through the front doors of the infirmary, looking panicked and desperate. Alli's parents walked out of Aiden's room and met them in the hall.

"Lily, is it true? Is Aiden my son?"

With tears flowing freely down her cheeks, Alli's mom just nodded and stepped aside allowing my dad to walk into Aiden's room.

"Go... go be with your dad. I think mine needs me right now, too. I will be right outside if you need me," Alli said.

Part of me wanted to, but part of me wasn't quite ready for all of this. In the end, I knew that Alli was right, so I took a deep breath, and walked into my brother's room.

Chapter 62

Allison

"I'm so happy to have my baby back," my mom said reaching over and squeezing me into a tight bear hug.

After Cade went in with his father to see Aiden, my mom and I came outside to get away from all the drama and get some air. It was freezing cold, but it was a welcome relief from the stifling confines of the little infirmary.

Pulling away from Mom a bit so that I could look her in the eye, I admitted, "I'm just not sure how to take this all in. How could you have never told us?"

Mom looked away as if it was too much to face me. "I don't know. You both were so young. And as more and more time passed, it felt like I had missed my chance to explain all of this. Dad was a dad to both of you, and he never saw Aiden as anything other than his son. To be honest, I guess I just took the easy way out by never telling you both the truth."

Again, she pulled me in for a hug and said, "I'm so sorry." Minutes passed before she spoke. "Can we talk about you and Cade?"

That completely threw me off. After all of this, she wanted to talk about me and Cade? "What is there to talk about?"

"Well, there's the fact that you two are true mates. Something that hasn't happened in a really long time. It's kind of a big deal. And you are so young, honey. You're mated and only seventeen. Don't you think that's worth talking about?"

I have never really thought about it like that. Mom was right. Seventeen is young, whether I wanted to admit it or not. It's like my life has suddenly been planned out for me. But… I loved Cade. And I couldn't imagine being without him.

"So what now, Mom? What happens next? We can't be apart. Are we like supposed to move in together?"

Before Mom could answer, Noel walked out and directly over to us. "Allison, can we talk?"

I looked over at my mom, not sure what to do. Honestly, Noel had never been anything but kind, but she still scared the hell out of me.

Immediately, Mom said, "I'll go back inside and let you two talk."

"No, Lillian. Please stay. We are all family now," Noel said.

Cade's mom sat down, and suddenly, I found myself sitting between two of the strongest, most self-assured women I have ever known. One who was the alpha-female of our pack and the one who was supposed to be.

Noel placed her hands over mine, which was totally weird, but I knew it was meant to be comforting. "Allison, first I want to apologize for my husband's behavior. He was completely out-of-line. He is the alpha, and he should have acted as one instead of a raging maniac. And if you tell him I said that, I'll adamantly deny it."

Her attempt at humor kind of lightened the mood. I did appreciate her apologizing for Marcus, but in my opinion, he was still a jerk. Alpha or not.

"You don't need to apologize, Mrs. Walker," I told her.

"Yes I do. You are family now. You are our son's mate. This is new for all of us, but I hope that we can get to know each other better." Then she looked over at my mom and said, "All of us. I want us all to be a family. And as the women in this family, we need to make sure that it happens. Our children are going to need us and our support."

Noel most definitely surprised me. The fact that she reached out to both my mother and me was kind of… unbelievable. I would have thought that she would be pissed, not to mention completely freaked out, about Aiden being Marcus's son, but she genuinely seemed okay with it. Not like it was no big deal, because it obviously was, but for her to take the news so well was shocking.

The door opened, and I felt Cade's presence before he even spoke. "Am I interrupting a female bonding moment?" We all turned and smiled.

Noel said, "Of course not, honey. Why don't Lillian and I give you two some time to talk?" She turned to my mom and asked, "What do you say, Lillian? Shall we go get a cup of coffee and check on Aiden?"

With a nod, my mom and Noel went inside leaving Cade and me alone. He walked over and sat down next to me. Instantly, my body temperature rose as he wrapped his arms around me.

"Allison, I know this is a lot to take in. Are you okay? Have you been checked out by Dr. Altman? I want to make sure you're alright."

"I'm fine really. My were-skin heals quickly," I joked, and then we laughed together at my own silly attempt to make light of our situation. "Stop worrying about me, Cade. How are you? What's going on in that head of yours? I know you must be a little shook up by the whole I-suddenly-have-a-brother thing," I continued.

"I don't want to talk about that now. I just want to know that you are okay. That's what matters most," he said.

We just sat there huddled together in the cold enjoying the feeling of being back in each other's arms before Cade spoke again. "I came so close to losing you. I don't know how I would have lived without you, Allison. I love you so much. You know that, right?" he asked with watery eyes.

I couldn't even speak. I wrapped my arms around his broad shoulders and pulled my mate's lips to mine, and in that moment, it all became clear. I never wanted to leave his side. Seventeen or seventy, it didn't matter. We were going to be together forever, and our forever was beginning right now.

I pulled away but only to say, "I love you too, Cade."

"I was hoping you would say that. You know, I found something, and I think it belongs to you." Cade stuck his hand in his pocket, pulled out his alpha ring, which now hung from a chain, and placed it around my neck. Where it would stay... forever.

Our lips found each other's again, and we kissed like we knew this was just the beginning of our new life together. Hearing the door behind us swing open, our lips parted. Marcus waved us over and said to us both, "Hurry in. Your brother is waking up!" Thank God I had Cade by my side because one thing was certain. Everything was about to change, not only for me and Cade, but for the entire Red Ridge Pack as well.

To be continued ...

Acknowledgments

We have to start by thanking our family for allowing us the time away from home to do what we love. Without their love and support, writing this book would have been impossible. To our beta reader, Shari Hassell, thanks for telling us how wonderful we are while pointing out all the mistakes we make. You make us sound like we know what we are doing.

We have to give a shout out to Patrick Golden for creating and updating our website, Jordan Mantell for his beautiful poetry, and our many supportive students that we have taught over the years.

Last, but certainly not least, a very special thanks to everyone at Boroughs Publishing Group. It was truly an honor having Jill Limber as our editor. We are so grateful that she saw something in our story that was worth passing along to Michelle. Both Jill and Michelle are the epitome of professionalism, and as fast as lightning!